## **Reflecting: Life as Mrs. Lance Brooks**

From her wedding day, we will find out what the former Morgan Hixon-Chambers has done the first year of her marriage in 2009. You'll be totally lost in this story if you didn't read the first part of The Reflections Series (Reflections: Journalizing the Life of Morgan Hixon-Chambers). Recap for those of you who may have forgotten or have no idea about this storyline:

Morgan Hixon-Chambers inherited an undisclosed amount of money from her late grandfather Willie James. She has a sister, Logan, who is her ultimate life source. From the time Morgan graduated high school and finished college, she did many unspeakable things all out of the fear of being hurt or having her heart broken. Not to mention letting Pandora's box filter out if anyone hurt anyone who meant something to her; especially Logan. Though wanting and seeking love, Morgan was afraid to allow love marinate her heart until the murder of her brother-in-law brought her to the man she would in turn marry. Her marred childhood often appeared as flashbacks in her sleep and a distorted yet somewhat evil presence of Morgan appeared only in mirrors. However in the end, Morgan was her own, worst enemy.

Now we pick up to all she experiences her first year of marriage.

# Reflecting:

## Life as Mrs.Lance Brooks

© ShayLa Bryant; 2014

## **<u>Acknowledgments and Appreciations</u>**

First, I'd like to thank God Almighty for giving me the talent, skill, and endurance to put together another installment of The Reflections Series. Without Him, I cannot do anything or make any of this possible. Giving all honor to God is mandate; no excuses, exceptions, or exchanges.

Second, much love to my family and friends. Whether you had supported me or not, I appreciate you all and I am blessed to have you all in my life.

Third, thank you to all who enjoyed the first book. The compliments and enthusiasm was more than I'd expected and I must truly say the eagerness for this book's release helped me keep the drive to entertain you all to the best of my ability.

# Introduction

I didn't know my first year of marriage was going to be a one of many twists and turns. A run in with my husband's ex, a confrontation with my mother, and somewhat of a past relationship damn near broke me down. Not to mention the biggest love of my life was no longer a part of my life. But this is me we're talking about. I still had nightmares of my childhood and I had to face an old relationship and expose more of my troubled past in college.

Facing major parts of my life I tried to suppress actually helped me heal. When I let out my demons, that distorted image of myself left me alone for good. Instead of me going to Logan as much as I used to, I learned to confide and lean more on my husband; especially when we had tragedy hit one of our children.

I had come to realize that life goes on and how I handle each situation was very critical. Acting out and being disruptive isn't the answer for everything. I had to stay blessed and breezy and the only way to do that was to stop holding on to pain and keep my life moving.

## **Chapter One**

May 14, 2009. I'm lying in the labor and delivery room contemplating on giving birth to my twins without asking for an epidural. I've already vomited twice bedside. Apparently, that's normal for some women just like it is normal for some women to move their bowels while pushing the baby out. All I know is this pain was nowhere what I expected from seeing Logan give birth to Austin; it was ten times worse. I breathed, huffed, puffed, moaned, and gripped and shook the bedrail with so much force that Lance tried rubbing my back to help me relax.

"That's not helping," I said in a low groan. "Just leave me alone."

"I can't," Lance answered. "I watched those other four of mine arrive in this world and I'm making sure I'm here every second these two come in."

I wished someone would've told me more in detail that labor felt like your reproductive system was about to do a spontaneous combustion; like your pelvic region was being reconstructed; all in all it was painful. At that point, I decided no natural childbirth for me. Nope. I needed drugs.

"Lance, get the anesthesiologist now. I can't do this anymore."

"Baby, you said—"

"I don't care what I said before! Go get the damn epidural person! This natural shit is overrated!"

Lance walked out of the labor and delivery room to look for the anesthesiologist or a nurse. I lied on my right side holding onto the bedrail as if my life depended on it. I heard the babies' heartbeats on the monitoring system and started thinking that this is it. I'm about to become a mother for the first and last time. It was all okay at first until my body began to feel as if it was being taken over by an alien life force. Think about it. Three people sharing one body for survival. We needed food, water, rest, exercise, and special attention. I couldn't sit down without rocking to get up, if I took a bath I had to call for help because my center of gravity was off, and I couldn't shave my legs or put socks on. Then there was the uncontrollable gas, five thousand trips to the bathroom, and my husband who still wanted to have playtime though my belly, hips, and thighs grown to enormous proportions. Nope. This is the first and last time I'd get pregnant. Just as I was calming down, another labor pain kicked in. I sat up and tried to rock the pain away and ended up making my water break. Finally! The Petocin I was given should've done that two hours ago and it didn't as the doctor had predicted. Then I was greeted by Lance, Dr. Langley (the anesthesiologist), and my nurse just as I wet the bed.

"Hello again, Mrs. Brooks," Dr. Langley said.

"Yeah, yeah, enough with the hellos. Stick me in my back please," I answered.

"Has anything happened since I was last in here?" the nurse asked.

"Yeah, my water broke about ten seconds ago."

"Oh, well let's check to see how far you've dilated before we give you the epidural," the nurse said. "I'll need you to lie back so I can get the doctor."

"What?!"

"I'm sorry, Mrs. Brooks, I can't give you the epidural if you're cervix is fully dilated," Dr. Langley answered.

"But I can't deal with this pain! Give me Demerol or something!"

"I'm sorry, but I have to see what Dr. Burrell says,"

"Damn it!" I exclaimed. "This is some bull—"

"Okay, Mo, okay. You're going to be fine," Lance reassured. He put his arms around me to help me lay back but I didn't

want to. But when a pain kicked in, I grabbed his head
hugged his neck and didn't realize I was suffocating him.
"Mo! Honey! You're squashing my nose against your body! I
can't breathe!" he muffled into my shoulder.
"I can't do this, Lance! I need drugs! Where's Dr. Burrell?!"
"I'm right here, dear," Dr. Burrell answered. She stood all of
five feet two inches and her pear shaped body was
exuberantly jolly. Her curly black hair was pulled up in a
ponytail as she walked to the baby monitoring systems. She
checked the contraction reader, the vital machines and
finally said, "I'm going to check you just as soon as I wash
and glove."
"Fine, but could you hurry it up?!" I asked.
Lance sat down in a chair away from me. He rubbed the
back of his neck with one hand and his face with the other.
"Dr. Burrell," he began, "I normally don't typically say this,
but, could you give her something before she kills me?"
The doctor smiled and put her gloves on as she walked over
to me. "I'll see what we can do after I check you. Okay, Mrs.
Brooks, I need you to spread out so I can see what the
dilation is now."
I did as I was instructed and allowed the doctor to make me
more uncomfortable by sticking her fingers inside my vagina
to check the cervix. With every poke and prod, it felt like a
burning needle with a lot of pressure and I had to bear
down while she measured.
"Okay, Mrs. Brooks," Dr. Burrell began, "you're now at 8
centimeters. I can't allow the epidural or Demerol. At the
rate you're going, these babies should be here within the
hour." She walked over to get the ultrasound wand and jelly
and applied it to my pregnant stomach. As she did so, we all
could see the images of the babies. One had its head down
and the other was in breech position.
"Hmmm," Dr. Burrell said, "looks like one baby wants to

stick around. Hopefully, he or she will turn around."

"What'll happen if he or she doesn't turn around?" Lance asked.

"We're going to have to manually turn the little one, wait for him or her to turn on their own, or...if it comes to worse, we may have to do a C-section," she answered.

"What?!" I asked. "I'm already here open, I can't get an epidural, and you're talking about cutting me after giving birth to one?!"

"Mo, calm down," Lance whispered. "Everything's going to be alright."

"This isn't you on this table going through hell. Shut up."

"Okay, okay. Do you want me to see where Logan is?"

"No. I just want the damn Demerol!"

"Well," Dr. Langley started, "I can't do that, Mrs. Brooks."

"This is some real bull!" I yelled.

For the next hour and a half, I groaned, winced, whined, and cried out in pain. Whoever said natural childbirth was beautiful was a damn lie! And how did women in the 19<sup>th</sup> and 20<sup>th</sup> century have 8, 9, or 10+ kids without drugs??? Why did they have that many? Lance gave me ice chips and called my sister so many times that it worried him that she didn't get there to calm *him* down. Logan, Brian, and the kids were in Floyd County visiting some of Brian's family and it was going to take them at least two hours to get to Fulton County Hospital. Finally, it was time to deliver the babies. With Lance standing to the right of me, he decided to hold my right hand and right thigh. It was the weirdest feeling to have all my business exposed with a doctor and two nurses watching too. The doctor instructed me to take a deep breath and push as if I were taking a dump. Every time, I counted to ten and had done that three times until Jayden made his entrance. Now I knew which

baby was head down. I heard his little cry and Dr. Burrell
held him up because I told her not to put the babies on me
while they were covered in goop. Lance kissed my forehead,
told me he loved me, and went over to cut the umbilical
cord. One nurse took Jayden over to the weighing table,
cleaned him up, and took his vitals.

"Lance," I began, "you wanna go over and see your son?"

"I can see him right where I am," he answered. "I want to
see Jayda."

It was weird because as soon as Jayden was out my pains
stopped, but Dr. Burrell looked concerned.

"What's going on?" I asked her.

"Your labor took a pause," she answered. "And it still looks
as if baby girl hasn't turned around. I have the placenta that
Jayden was in and everything looks okay here, but I have to
try to get her to move."

Lance began to rub my stomach again. "C'mon, Jayda," he
said. "You have to come out."

Dr. Burrell picked up the ultrasound wand and jelly again
and saw the baby was still facing the wrong way.

"She's too far up in the uterus and her placenta hasn't
broken," she stated.

"Wait," I started, "they both weren't in the same bag?"

"Nope," she answered. "You have fraternal twins and they
had their own little homes. I'm going to break your water
this time because your uterus seemed to slow down with
contracting."

I immediately started thinking that this little girl was going
to be the death of me as she got older. She was determined
to hang around and make me miserable. Lance began to
worry. I knew he was because he started biting his bottom
lip and grip my hand firmly.

"Go over and see Jayden," I suggested to him.

"I can't leave you," he whispered.

"I'm not going anywhere, sweetie," I reassured. "Just go check on our son."

Lance looked at me and hesitated. After about ten seconds, he kissed my cheek and walked over to Jayden. I saw my husband over with the baby watching and waiting to hold him. Then, I felt my heart palpitate rapidly before I went into a deep sleep.

\*\*\*\*\*\*\*\*\*\*\*\*\*\*\*\*\*\*\*\*\*\*\*\*\*\*\*\*\*\*\*\*\*\*\*\*\*\*\*\*\*\*\*\*\*\*\*\*\*\*\*\*

It's early in the afternoon I'm lying across my bed thinking what am I going to do now? I hope that what I did was from too much drinking. Then again, I hope it was a dream or a ten year long deep dark coma. God, what are you trying to tell me? Have I really become a big screw up?

I roll over and get up outta bed, walk outta my bedroom door. Go across the hallway and into my bathroom and closed the door. Just before I turn on bathwater I heard a knock on the mirror. I was startled at what I saw. That reflection couldn't be any clearer!

It's a woman the same color as me with the same eyes as mine. That smile looked familiar; facial features exactly like mine. The only difference was the voice I heard from that reflection in front of me that got closer and closer. It scared me so much I almost couldn't breathe.

"Why are you so afraid of what's in front of you? No need to coward up now. It's time you see what I've been through."

I couldn't believe my reflection was bringing my life in front of me. Making me see things from a different way; things I just didn't wanna see.

"Remember at 16 you lost your virginity? Then vowed to never do it again? But, you met your high school love and thought your love would never end.

Your mama took you away to a place that was just a living hell. So to defy her and your soul you turned into someone who shouldn't have been alive and well. You broke out of your shell and dressed more provocative. You didn't give a damn about school it was your life; your prerogative. You found power in your beauty and took it to an advantage. Had guys bending over backwards for you; then one had proposed marriage.

Being young and foolish and not realizing the consequences, you accepted and married secretly not even knowing his intentions. After he tried to beat and rape you and keep you under surveillance, you ran off and filed for divorce, and you crumpled up in an evil trance. From that point on, no man got close; no matter the amount of gifts.

You became the woman you hated. Therefore, you became the ultimate bitch. Talking to men seductively, going out on a couple of dates, screwing the hell out of them, and then tossing them aside at alarming rates. Never letting anyone get close to your heart because you knew that's all you had. As a child you were molested and denied the chance to know your dad. So why get hurt again by another man...to hell with that! I'm gonna take as long as I can; I deserve to give every ounce of pain back!

You took one man's money; took another man's car. Accepted the fact you lost yourself; being deceptive just went too far. Even became like your boys; looking for anonymous pieces just to get laid. Then decided to take it elsewhere; you used dumb girls to get you paid. Weed was your outlet and liquor became your best friend. Time on and then time over again you asked for your life to end.

So, you decided to settle down with three complete fools no good to you and who did you the same way you treated all the men who you screwed. Now, you're all alone again looking at this reflection in front of you. You're trying to figure out about your life. What it is you wanna do?"

What do I wanna do? What the hell does that question mean? Then again, I'm confused I need more clarity.

"Do you wanna be a nobody or a somebody with a prosperous life? Do you wanna keep whoring? Or accepting to prepare to become a child of God? Do you wanna be a child or raise a child of your own? Do you wanna live healthy and happy or continue to be sadly alone? What is wrong with you? What the fuck is on your mind? You're a beautiful, gifted woman; why did you do what you did last night?!"

Then, that reflection went away and right then I remembered the night before. Oh, please forgive me, God... Then I had a knock at the front door. I came outta the bathroom and walked down the hall; looked out the peephole. The face looked familiar to me and all of a sudden, my body got cold. I unlocked the door and opened it just only a little bit. That man outside my door; for some reason just didn't feel legit.

He said, "What's going on, Baby Girl! Why'd you leave me last night?"
I said, "I had to come home. I wasn't really feeling alright."
"Well can I come in a minute? I wanna sit and talk to you?"
"No maybe another time. I have so many things I gotta do."
"Woman, I ain't going nowhere so you better let me in right now!"
"Man have you lost your mind?! You ain't gettin' in; no way, no how!"

I tried to close my door, but it was too late. This man pushed the door open and grabbed me up by the face. While kicking the door shut, he smiled and grinned at me. Now I remember who this man was...I took his life he gave to me.

"I gave you my money, let you have the car to drive. Even opened my heart to you. Nevertheless, you slept with my friend and I don't know why! I was so stupid with you; ten years, two kids, and you're still the same. While making love to me, you were whispering my brother's name! Well, woman, whatcha gotta say 'cause this shit's ending right now! You see, you're time is up, Baby Girl. I'm not letting you go alive; no way no how!"

Before I could say a word, I felt this burning pain that hit my chest in two places; one in my neck and two in my brain. Then nothing but darkness; my breathing began to slow down.

**************************************************

"Morgan, baby, wake up!" I heard a voice very muffled say to me. I couldn't open my eyes as much as I tried because the sleep I was in felt too good. Peaceful.
"C'mon, Mo, wake up! Wake up!" It was Lance.
"Please, Mr. Brooks, you have to stay out of the room," I heard a voice say. "We have to try to keep her stable."
"I can't go! Morgan, I love you! Wake up, please!" Lance yelled.
"Lance, stop yelling," I whispered.
"Wait, wait! She just said something!" Lance declared.
I finally opened my eyes to reassure my husband I was awake. But that awful dream I had; was it real? Did I really do those things? Or was it a premonition?
"Mrs. Brooks, this is Dr. Burrell," the doctor said. "Can you hear me?"
"Yes," I answered. "Why is everyone yelling? Why do I have this mask on my face?" I finally opened my eyes and noticed I was no longer in the labor and delivery room. Lance was walking over to me and kissed my forehead. A nurse injected me with something in my IV and there was a sheet up in front of me that kept me from seeing anything past my chest.

"What's going on?" I asked. "Why can't I feel my legs or abdomen?"

Lance sat next to me, grabbed my right hand and started bawling which was a sight and sound unfamiliar to me. Then I noticed Dr. Langley was to my left.

"Mrs. Brooks, you gave us quite a scare," she said. "However, we need you to try to stay awake. We'll explain everything once you're in your room."

"Baby, my beautiful baby," Lance cried. "Oh, God I thank you for bringing her back to me. Thank you, Father!"

"Lance..." I couldn't say anything more. Just from that statement, I knew what I didn't want to know.

Later that evening, I was in my hospital room with both of my babies, Lance, Logan, Brian, and all their kids. My step-children had just left and went home. I had two different IV tubes stuck to me and I was on a vital monitor. There was a catheter inserted into me as well and I was still trying to move my legs which instantly made me paranoid.

"Why can't I move my legs?!" I asked.

"You were given an epidural for the C-section," Lance answered.

"Can someone please explain to me what happened?"

Lance hesitated. He tried but his eyes welled up with tears. Logan, who sat on my left side holding a pink blanket containing Jayda said, "Mo, your blood pressure shot up out of nowhere and you slipped into a mini coma. You were on the brink of a heart attack."

"You flat-lined on us," Lance said with his voice still breaking up. "We almost lost you. You had to get an emergency C-Section after you were stabilized enough to have the procedure done. But I was told I would've had to make the hardest decision in my life if you didn't wake up."

"Which was?" I asked.

Lance didn't want to answer. I saw him swallow hard. He still had on the scrubs over his black t-shirt and blue jeans. "They were telling me to choose between saving your life or Jayda's life. I told them I'm not choosing either one of you because I wanted both of you to live. Baby, you died for about two minutes."

I was speechless. So the whole time I was dreaming, I was actually dead...wow. But that dream, it felt so real. Everything was too familiar; my mirror image speaking to me, the burn from bullets entering my body, and the man who shot me. I've seen his face before. What was all of that though? Was it my life flashing before me? But it couldn't have been because I wasn't married ten years and half of what my reflection told me wasn't true.

"Mo?" Logan questioned me out of my thoughts. "Are you okay? I know this is a lot for you to digest."

"Umm, yeah," I replied. "I'm okay." Then it hit me; I haven't held either of my babies yet. I scanned the room and saw Brian was holding Jayden. I waved to get his attention until he looked up. Even though he had his hearing aids on I signed to him, "Can you bring me my baby please?"

"Sure," Brian answered vocally. He got up out of the chair that was surrounded with their kids gawking at the baby and walked over to me. Brian carefully passed my son to me and I was in complete awe. This was my son! A little boy who was going to grow up and look to me as the model of who he should look for in a wife someday. Yes, I was already projecting that future. His little light brown face had a dimple in each cheek. His eyes and nose were just like Lance's and he had straight little strains of black hair all over his head.

"Hi, Jayden," I whispered as I nuzzled his little face. "I'm your mommy. I'm glad I finally get to hold you and I promise I'll never let you go." Jayden opened one eye and looked at me then closed it. It was as if he was saying he had his eye on me. He eventually opened both eyes and I melted. His little wrinkly hands were balled up into fists close to his chest and the baby smell just engulfed me. Lance sat next to me and leaned in to give us both kisses. "He weighed in at five pounds and seven ounces," Lance said. "And Jayda weighed in at five pounds and ten ounces." "Cookie, give me Jayda," I ordered. "I need to hold both of them." I shifted Jayden in my right arm so Logan could put his sister in my left. She was the total opposite of her brother as far as looks go. She was just as high yellow as I am, had a head full of curly light brown hair that it almost looked blonde, yet she had that same nose and mouth as Lance's. Her face was fuller and she was so bright-eyed; looking at me with intensity.

"Hello, Jayda," I began. "I'm your mommy. Just as your big brother, I'm glad I finally get to hold you and I promise you I'll never let you go." I don't know if she understood me, but I received the cutest toothless smile from her and I smiled from ear to ear. Everyone said 'Aww' at the same time. Brian walked to the front of the hospital bed and said, "Bro, lean in closer so I can get a picture of y'all."

Lance leaned in but decided to hold Jayden while I held Jayda. Brian took a picture with his digital camera and sat down. I looked over at my husband, whose face lit up brighter than a Christmas tree, and was relieved that God gave me a second chance to be amongst those I loved the most. Lance leaned in further to me and said some words that I wasn't ready for. "Morgan, from the first time I laid my eyes on you, I knew someday you were going to be mine. I know that we were both in relationships and how we met was really messed up, but I knew you were going to be my wife and mother to my children. When we were first alone, I knew at that moment why it was never meant for me to marry Sharayne; no matter how many times I asked her or settled for that life. You were made specifically for me and I'll never take you for granted. I'm just thankful God brought you back to me and from this day forth, I vow to love you each day as if it were our last day together." I couldn't say a word and there was nothing I had to say. Lance leaned his head close enough for me to give him the biggest kiss I could while we held our babies. From that exchange, I felt something deep in the pit of my stomach that was unlike any other kiss I'd received from Lance. I sensed relief, love, appreciation, and commitment from him just from a kiss.

"Okay, now, there are kids in the room," my nephew A.J. stated.

"Boy, hush," Logan replied. "With all the little scallywags chasing you, it wouldn't surprise me if you haven't been kissing some of them."

"A.J. has two girlfriends, Mommy," Amira signed and vocalized. Amira was receiving speech therapy since she had received a cochlear implant and Brian helps her out a lot too by teaching her how to lip-read. A.J. had just turned 12 two months prior, Amira was coming up to her 10th birthday in July, Aleasha was approaching her 6th birthday in June, and we were a week away from Austin's 4th birthday. A.J. was looking more and more like his late father Amari. He had the same pronounced cheekbones, broad jaw line, widow's peak, and thick jet black hair which he kept in braids. Ever since little girls at his school said they liked the way he danced like Omarion, that's who he had been trying to emulate. Amira was the same shade of mahogany as her brother and was almost as tall as he was. Her almost impossible to comb thick hair was straightened with a hot comb and pulled back into a ponytail. For a while, Lance's mother questioned Amira's paternity once it got back to her that Logan had an affair. Logan was afraid because she wasn't sure herself. She finally got enough courage to get the DNA testing by using Lance's mom as the specimen giver. Though her late husband, Amari Sr, and Lance were brothers, it was better to get her DNA because Lance and Amari Sr. had two different fathers. Lo and behold, Amira did share the Brooks' genes and a sigh of relief swept over Logan as it did with me because Lance's mom can be ruthless sometimes. Now, Aleasha and Austin could've been identical twins. Both of them looked like Brian with the same curly hair, blue eyes, and smile. Their hair color became darker the older they got and their noses were the same as Logan's. If Aleasha didn't have earrings and wore girly clothes, you almost couldn't tell her from Austin from a distance.

"Well, A.J.," I started, "you be careful who you kiss. You might get more than cooties nowadays."

"For real? Like what?" his preteen raspy voice asked.

"Herpes, meningitis..." Logan answered.

"What's that?" A.J. asked. "Do you get it from open or closed mouth kissing?"

"Well, well, well," Lance chimed in. "It seems we've opened Pandora's Box, A.J."

"Yeah," Brian added. "Looks like we need to have a talk. Oh...I do have my aids on and I can hear everything loud and clear."

For the rest of the evening, we all took turns feeding, holding, and changing the babies. Lance and Brian went out to grab some pizzas and sodas for everyone except me. I couldn't eat all of that considering what happened. The doctors and nurses were urging everyone to leave so I could rest, but I rebutted that all of the way until visiting hours were over. I did notice that Lance was very irritated at around 7:30 that evening. He kept checking his phone and would periodically walk out of the room when his phone rang. When Brian, Logan, and their kids left an hour later, I asked Lance what was going on. He told me he was checking on the whereabouts of his kids and why they didn't get here before visiting hours were over.

"They knew how much this meant to us for them to be here," Lance said.

"Honey, it's okay. You can't expect them to come see their step-mother and their new siblings because you want them to," I replied.

"What's that supposed to mean?" Lance asked as he walked Jayda over to her hospital issued baby crib next to Jayden's. His black t-shirt was clinging tightly to his muscular upper torso and his biceps flexed as he gently put the baby down. For Lance to be approaching 40 years of age, he kept his body in tact like a 20 year old.

"It means you have young adults on your hands," I replied.

"Sweetheart, Keenan is 19 and I'm sure he's in no hurry to see two babies that could be his own. Lamar, Alanna, and Chantel are doing what teenagers do. Don't rush it or they'll resent you later."

"Mo, it's the principle of coming together as a family and welcoming our newest additions to the Brooks' lineage. Don't make excuses for them."

Lance's cell phone rang and he immediately answered.

"Hello? Keenan, where are y'all? I told you to be here hours ago...what...*what?!*...when?...where are you now?...why didn't you call me to tell me this before?...alright, alright. Just go home and I'll see you all in the morning...Okay...yeah, you and Lamar come after your sisters go to school in the morning. Alright."

"Well, what was all that about?" I asked.

Lance pulled up the roll-a-way bed as close to me as

possible the hospital furnished for him so he could sleep over. Considering he was adamant about not leaving my side after this ordeal and the birth of the babies, Lance wasn't being moved by anyone. He looked at me very hesitant to tell me what was going on with his children. "It's too much to get into," he exhaled. "Besides...you've been through enough today. Come to think of it, I should've asked Logan and her crew to come back tomorrow. I'm sorry, Mo. I wasn't thinking."

"No, it's okay," I said. "You know how much you all mean to me. I'm glad everyone was here despite what happened."

"Yeah, but all of the excitement could've had you relapse—"

"But it didn't. I know you've been monitoring me just like the nurses and the doctors. And if it weren't for this constant drip of pain medication to keep me mellow, I would've been set off hours ago. Lance...I'm sleepy now."

"Enough said. Don't worry about the babies. I have them...unless you want to breast feed."

"Umm...I'll pass. I'm not comfortable with taking drugs and feeding that to the babies."

"Okay. Goodnight, Mo."

"Backatcha."

As much as I wanted to tell Lance my dream, I decided not to. I had to understand it for myself before I shared this with him. So instead, I drifted off to sleep listening to soft music Lance brought to me from home.

Around 6am, I was awakened by the nurse assigned to me during the nightshift. She wanted to take my vitals and check on the babies. Lance was balled up under the hospital blankets given to him sleeping peacefully. The short, black-haired nurse wrote down in my chart all of my information from the vitals. With her straight hair pulled pack with a hair comb, the pale, freckle-faced woman wearing pink scrubs said to me, "You're looking good, Mrs.

Brooks. Your blood pressure has been stable for the past 12 hours and your sugar levels are normal. Is there anything I can do for you before the nurse on the next shift take over?" I scoot back in my bed a little and said, "Yes. Can I please have some ice water or Gatorade? I'm very thirsty."

"I can get some water for you," she answered. "Not sure about the Gatorade yet. Dr. Burrell will be in shortly along with the cardiologist."

"Okay, thanks," I replied. I had the feeling back in my legs and was able to move feet. It's the weirdest feeling to not have any control over body movements or being able to make your limbs move after they've been made to sleep by medication. I noticed that the twins were moving around so I attempted to get out of bed to tend to them.

"What are you doing?" Lance asked as he shifted in the roll away bed looking at me.

"I thought you were sleeping," I responded.

"Girl, let me get the babies."

"I'm tired of lying down."

"Not an option." Lance suggestively put his hands on my shoulders for me to stay put. "Besides, you're still hooked to a catheter."

"That's what that nagging tug is!" I said. "I knew something didn't feel right."

"You mean you couldn't feel a tube in between your thighs?"

"I'm partially numb. There's a lot I can't decipher."

"I understand." Lance reached in to pick up Jayda first. Typical. I laughed and he asked what was funny.

"Gotta get daddy's little girl first," I answered.

"Ha. Whatever. She's the one that slept a little longer than her brother. So I figured she's going to need attention first. Jayden kept me up until around 3:30 this morning."

"Really? Wow. What was he doing?"

"He needed changing three times, wanted to eat, and

wanted me to talk to him. He kept me busy. Little man was busy. Jayda was fed and changed and went to sleep around two in the morning." Lance brought Jayda over to me and she had her eyes wide open. Her pink hat covered her curly mane and she was moving her head and opening her mouth looking to eat. "Hey, ma'am," I said to her. "You need a middle name. Since your father picked your first name, I get the pleasure of giving you a middle name." I gestured for a bottle of ready-made formula from Lance who was already holding Jayden.

"Just don't name her something frivolous. Or ghetto or corny or—"

"Shut up, will you? I got this," I rebutted. I kept looking at my daughter searching for the right name. I was so in awe that she was one of the babies I was carrying that I stopped thinking about her name. She just had the baby smell. You know...the smell every baby has once they're newborns. It smelled like heaven and I enjoyed every whiff. Then it hit me. "Your name is Jayda Renee Brooks." Lance looked over at me then looked at his baby girl.

"I like that," he said. "I like that a lot. And this little guy is..."

"Jayden Michael Brooks," I said. "I knew his name when I held him yesterday."

A knock was on the room door and entered Dr. Burrell and a man that I guessed was the cardiologist. He was tall with dark features, streaks of gray hair on his temples, and quite handsome. He wore some wire frame glasses and had a pearly white smile. He introduced himself to Lance first before me.

"Good morning," the doctor said to me with a very deep, yet melodic voice. "My name is Dr. Salvatore and I was involved with treating you yesterday. How are you doing this morning, Mrs. Brooks?"

I didn't want to answer because I was afraid I had morning

breath. Hesitantly I said, "I'm better. Can't wait for this catheter to go and I'm starting to get feeling back."

"Good," Dr. Salvatore said. "So I want to go over some things with you and run some more tests before we determine if you can go home in a few days."

"A few days?" I inquired. "Why not today?"

"We need to observe you a little more; just as a precaution," he answered.

"So what happened to my wife?" Lance interjected.

"We believe Morgan was under extreme stressful labor which caused the angina," Dr. Burrell answered. "Her body was working triple time to have two babies. This happens to many women and shouldn't be taken lightly. However, it tends to spike when a woman is already anxious."

"What do you mean?" I asked.

"You were very upset when you couldn't get the anesthesia—"Dr. Burrell began.

"Are you saying this was *my* fault?!" I asked.

"No," Dr. Salvatore answered. "What Dr. Burrell is saying is because you were already tense and uncomfortable and wanted meds, your body went into overdrive. Now, from the tests we ran so far, your small heart attack was stress induced. Otherwise, your heart valves don't show any blockages from plague build-up, there are no tears or scars, or anything where you would need to have open heart surgery or stints put into place."

"Thank God," Lance said. "So what should we do from here to keep her from getting to this point again?"

"Morgan is going to have to be very careful not to get worked up for the next several weeks. I take it you're going to be on maternity leave and that should be enough time to properly rest and maintain stability," Dr. Burrell answered.

"You scared me, young lady. Your husband made it even worse on me because he made me promise to try to save both of you. But I couldn't have done anything without Dr. Salvatore's assistance. He happened to be on his way home when he was found walking by the OR by one of my nurses." Dr. Burrell's pear-shaped body moved closer to me to press on my abdomen and to check the incision after she washed and gloved her hands. "Are you still numb from the epidural for the C-section?"

"A little. This is funny," I said wincing from the pressure, "all of that I went through to get the epidural and I received one anyway. I was able to move my legs and feet finally. When can this catheter be taken out?"

"Well, if you can feel your legs and feet, you should be able to get up to use the bathroom," she answered. "You can continue to hold that precious little darling while I do this." Jayda stopped drinking her formula so I put her up on my shoulder to burp her. While I was doing that, Dr. Salvatore spoke with Lance who had a million and one questions. Dr. Burrell pulled the curtain for privacy so she could remove the catheter from my urethra. It was quite uncomfortable too. Jayda burped twice and that heavenly baby smell kept me distracted anyway.

"Dr. Burrell, thank you so much for everything," I said. "No problem," she replied. "Listen, Morgan...you really need to take it easy for a while. Make that fine husband of yours work his ass off!" We laughed together in agreement. One thing I could say about Dr. Burrell is that she was the best doctor I've ever had in my adult life. She was down to earth and treated me like a person; not a number or a case. As she pulled the curtain, back I laid Jayda on the blanket I had over my shoulder used to burp her so I could change her diaper. Dr. Salvatore told me he would see me later on after the tests he ordered were administered and after that, both of the physicians left. Lance and I traded babies for a while so I can get my time with my son. It was weird for me to say that I had a son and daughter for a while, but not weird for me to get used to. At that point, I totally understood what it meant for a woman to fall in love with her children. All I wanted to do was snuggle them and I did that all day while I was awake.

Three days later, I was able to go home. The babies and I were welcomed home to the most warming environment. The house was clean, their nursery (which was Keenan's old room) was redone by Chantel and Alanna, and Lance set up the most amazing chef to cook for us for the next two weeks. He also hired the woman who typically does my pedicures to come to the house to hook up my feet. Pastor and Mrs. Isaacs came to visit along with some of my co-workers from Shining Star, some of Lance's co-workers, and of course my sister Logan and her family. It was a wonderful homecoming and I thank God for making all of that possible through my loving family He blessed me with. If only things stayed that calm the weeks to follow...

## Chapter Two

August 2009. It was two days after Lance's 39th birthday and we had just come back from a weekend getaway to celebrate it with no kids or other distractions. The babies were three months old and I think it was the perfect time to regroup and get back to one-on-one time. On the drive back home, we listened to a mix CD that Lance made and Howard Hewitt's song *Show Me* started playing in the car. He knew how much I loved that song and started to sing along.

"Uh...no...don't mess this up," I said.

"Psh, girl you know you love to hear me sing," Lance stated.

"Yeah, but not on my favorites."

"Mmm....okay. Thank you for that wonderful weekend. This'll be a birthday to add to most memorable."

"You're welcome. Besides...all work and no play makes you a cranky-spanky."

"No. You mean all work and no play for in the car. He knew how much I loved that song and started along.

"Uh...no...don't mess this up," I said.

"Psh, girl you know you love to hear me sing," Lance stated.

"Yeah, but not on my favorites. You do better accapella."

"Mmm....okay. Thank you for that wonderful weekend. This'll be a birthday to add to most memorable."

"You're welcome. Besides...all work and no play makes you a cranky-spanky."

"No. You mean all work and no play for *you* makes you cranky." Lance's cell phone rang. "Mo, answer that for me."

I picked up the phone and flipped it open. "Hello?"

"Can I speak to Lance?" a woman's voice asked. It was Sharayne his ex-girlfriend and mother to his first four children.

"Umm...excuse me?" I retorted.

"Oh, hi Morgan," the hoarse voiced woman said. "Congrats on your babies, by the way."

"Yeah...thanks," I said. "What do you want with Lance? He's busy right now and I can relay the message."

"Hmph. It sounds like you're trying to monitor his phone calls like he's a child."

"Or maybe keep him from childish interactions like the one we're having now." Lance shook his head. He knew who was on the other end. "What do you want me to tell him, Sharayne?"

"Well, I was going to ask him if he could give me Chantel's cell number again since she keeps changing it."

"No problem; 404-555-9311." I answered.

"Oh...thank you." Then I noticed the call dropped.

"Mo, I'm sorry—"

"What's the point of her calling you?"

"For Chantel and Alanna."

"They're 16 and 15 years old, Lance. That's bullshit."

"But that's still their mother and sometimes I'd like to keep her posted on how they are."

"Let her call them and they call her. They're not babies or small children anymore. They both have jobs and a social life. And from what I was told by Chantel, she could care less if she heard or seen Sharayne."

Lance drove quietly for a while. I knew when I struck a chord with him because he would just be quiet. But the look on his face said something different to me.

"Are you upset?" I inquired.

"No," he answered.

"How long have you been talking to her prior to today?"

Lance quickly glanced at me and then back at the road.

"What are you talking about?"

I looked at him while I turned the car stereo completely off.

"Do you have any idea how I feel when she's calling you to

talk about half-grown children all of a sudden?"

"Mo, you're reading too much into this. You know what was going on with our kids after they moved here with us; especially with Keenan. His situation got out of hand for a while in college dealing with those girls and you and I agreed that we needed to intervene while we could."

"I understand that and yes I did agree. However, *you* decided to include his mother after Keenan didn't want her involved with his life. Do you have any idea what it's like for me dealing with her calling you about you all's children? How it sounds to hear her condescending tone of her voice that flows through the other end of the phone? Do you have any idea what it's like for me to constantly have to put up with Sharayne calling you about *Keenan*??!!" I yelled.

"Mo, c'mon. What do you want me to do? She's still a part of my life because I have four kids with her!" Lance responded.

"Correction. You *had* four kids with her! You two share half-grown children now. You don't have any obligations to her! You have obligations with me, Jayden, and Jayda! She messed up and passed you by; I didn't! So she doesn't need to be calling here on some bull about Keenan's lifestyle that she don't like!"

"Morgan, do you hear yourself right now? You're sounding like a jealous, insecure woman!"

"Jealous and insecure? Nigro...please! Fed up with her nonsense is what it is! Don't you get it? She's trying to see how *we* live, what *we* do, so *she* could get you back!"

"I don't want her! I'm committed to you!"

"Oh really? Then tell her to back off with all of the camaraderie. It's not welcomed here in this house or on your phone! Your kids are half-grown and whether you see this or not...game recognize game and she's about to go into overtime with me!"

"You know, you really messed up our weekend getaway with

this conversation right about now. One minute, we're feeling good, floating on cloud nine, and you want to argue about my past. But the moment I want to discuss *your* past, to try to understand *you* better, you completely change to subject, disregard it! Newsflash, Mo...I know you have a lot of garbage you've done before we got together and one of these days, God forbid, we're going to be in a situation where your past is going to come to you in full circle. Sad thing is no one will be able to set you free from it except me! Now...put the music back on. We have nothing else to discuss and I don't want to hear your voice right now."
I looked at him and felt every muscle in my body tense up ready to punch him in the face. But I knew if I had done that, all hell would've broken loose. So I crossed my arms and looked out of the window at the scenery on the interstate. Then I started thinking about what Lance said on how my past coming back to me in full circle. That's not what I want at all. I had come this far without dealing with my past and once I decided to let it go, that's where I wanted to leave it; especially since I had that dream, or nightmare, when I lost consciousness having the babies. I was still trying to figure out if that was real or if it wasn't.

We arrived back home in Alpharetta two hours after our argument. We pulled up in the driveway in complete silence. I got out of Lance's 2012 white on white Trail Blazer and walked to the side door of the house. It felt so good to be home and welcomed by the sounds of music playing in our living room upon entering the threshold. Though Chantel and Alanna had agreed to watch the twins, I knew it would've been better to have Logan be on watch just in case they became too much for them. After all, they were 15 and 16 years old. Logan and her girls were in the living room with the babies and Chantel. Chantel was holding her baby sister and Jayda was just as content.

"Hey, Mo-Ma!" Chantel greeted. My step-children gave me that name because they said I had been more of a mother to her than their own, but didn't want to disrespect Sharayne by calling me mom. I understood and accepted it. Chantel stood up in her red leisure-wear that she only wore at home; a short sleeved shirt with matching capris made out of cotton blend material. Her very curvy body often drew unwanted attention from boys and her father and brothers always try to do a wardrobe check before she leaves the house. She kept a short, curly coif and her light brown skin was unblemished. Chantel looked somewhat like her mother, but more attractive because she had a blend of her father's features. Keenan often gets into a lot of fights with guys because of her whenever he comes home from college. While he was in high school, he was constantly bullying boys and intimidating them about Chantel. Whenever Lamar came home from college, he couldn't wait to chaperone his little sisters around and hang out with them. His bond with Chantel and Alanna was stronger than Keenan's bond with them. I think it was because Lamar knew that his little sisters were becoming young women and no matter how much he didn't like guys gawking at them, he had to make them feel loved and respected. Keenan, on the other hand, didn't like the fact that other men could possibly be womanizers like he was.

Anyway, Chantel stood up off of the couch with Jayda and walked over to me and gave me a hug.

"How was you and Dad's weekend?" she asked.

"It was wonderful," I answered. "How was yours?"

"No problem," she replied. "Auntie Lo decided her and the girls would stay over so it became a sleepover. We've been having fun!"

"Really? What have y'all been doing?" I reached for Jayda, whose little, round 3 month old body was dressed in a multi-print onesie with her curly hair all over her head. She smelled like the pink baby lotion and my nose took in that heavenly scent. As I kissed those chunky cheeks, Jayda smiled.

"Well, Amira and Aleasha had been teaching me more sign language, we were playing board games, watching movies, dancing, and of course my favorite...runway modeling." Chantel wanted to become a professional model to represent curvy women. She actually got a few agencies looking to have her as a client, but Lance refuses to sign consent.

"Sounds like y'all did have a ball," I stated. "How were the babies?"

"Sis, they were no problem," Logan said walking to me to give me a hug. "They have got to be the quietest 3 month olds I've ever known." Logan smiled from ear to ear as she held Jayden. She had her hair in micro twists that hung past her shoulders and was dressed in her favorite summertime attire; brown sandals that matched her brown spaghetti-strapped sundress. Since having the four kids, Logan's body put on 50 pounds to the once 125 pound body post-high school. But she looked good and filled out proportionately.

"Thank you," I said. "How often did you put them down? I know how much you loved to hold your babies; even while they slept."

Logan laughed, "Mo, I promise I didn't hold them as much as I'd like to. I know how you and Lance are sticklers for not coddling them a lot."

"Good," I said.

"But Aleasha and Amira stayed on them," Chantel said.

"Where are they anyway?" I asked.

"In my room watching Madagascar," Chantel replied.

"Hey...where's my dad?"

"Probably still outside pissed at me," I said.

"Huh?" Logan asked. "What happened? I thought you said you had a wonderful weekend?"

"We did until a phone call came through two hours ago," I replied. Chantel walked out to her father. I knew she was going to see what happened. Though she and I have bonded, she is still a Daddy's Girl.

"Hmm, let me guess...Sharayne," Logan said.

"Yup," I concurred.

"What now?" Logan inquired.

"She wanted Chantel's cell phone number."

"So..."

"So the problem is she's constantly calling Lance on some lame excuse with their half-grown kids. Chantel's changing her cell phone number, Keenan's running around with different women, Lamar's breaking his promises to her, and Alanna don't want to deal with her at all...I mean she made her bed with her kids; not Lance. It's a little late to try to reach out and be a commendable mother now, don't you think?"

"Mo, is it possible that you're holding on to bad feelings for *our* mother that you can't see Sharayne is trying to right the wrongs of her past with *her* children?"

"What?! No!"

Jayden's light brown, round baby body was nestled against Logan's bosom trying to fall to sleep.

"Mo, let's be real, okay? You still hold our mother accountable for a lot of the recklessness in your life. And the moment you see a mother/daughter relationship just as dysfunctional as ours was, you immediately side with the daughter and blame the mother for the daughter's pain. Have you ever thought that maybe the daughter may have been the cause of the dysfunction?"

"What has Alanna and Chantel done that you would consider dysfunctional? Huh?"

"Not only them. I'm talking about some of your clients at Shining Star. C'mon, Mo. As some point you're going to have to address this issue instead of avoiding it."

"Why? Because you did?"

"This has nothing to do with me."

"Why did you bring this up? I already had a rough time on the way home with my husband."

Logan walked to Jayden's bassinette to lay him down since he fell asleep. Jayda was still awake and I walked over to the oversized couch to sit down with her. Logan sat across from me in the recliner. She took a deep breath and moved some of her braids from the front of her face to the back.

"Mo, Grandmama called. There's a situation going on up there and I've been thinking of going back up there for a while to help her out."

"What kind of situation?"

"She just doesn't sound the same. Like she's sick or sad."

"You're going to uproot everyone and go back up to Pittsburgh?"

"No. I was just going to go for about two to three months. I've discussed this with Brian and he said he'd be okay with the kids while I went."

"But what about your job?"

"I'd be able to work from there using my laptop. You know...you should come too."

"Oh, I don't think I can. I mean, things here have come full circle for me; my career, my family...my peace of mind."

"But it's Grandmama, Mo."

I took a deep breath. I loved that woman more than anyone else on this earth because she took me in and made sure I was cared for at the most vulnerable time of my life.

"Let me discuss this with Lance. I'm pretty sure he won't

have a problem with this. I'd just have to let the CEO of Shining Star know about the leave of absence I want to take."

"Cool. I'm going to get the girls and head home. I have heads to do for school tomorrow and that's a task all in itself." Logan stood up and walked down the hallway to Chantel's bedroom. I continued to sit on the couch and held Jayda. She held on to my finger as she and I gazed at each other. "God, please help me be the best mother I can be for my daughter and son," I prayed out loud.

Lance and Chantel walked in the house carrying our luggage. Chantel carried my things to my bedroom and Lance stopped abruptly to detour over to me and Jayda. He sat his luggage down by the couch to peer over Jayden before he sat next to me. He looked at me suggesting that he wanted his baby girl so I handed her over. His face lit up as she smiled the closer he got to his face. Lance kissed and hugged Jayda as if he hadn't seen her in a lifetime. She cooed from the exchange and Lance began to sit back on the couch more. He positioned the baby in his right arm and put his left hand on my thigh.

"Mo, I love you and I'm sorry for snapping at you."
I said nothing. I sat there and gazed at the wall. What I really wanted to say, I held back. I learned from Mrs. Isaacs that the worse thing a wife can do to her husband is emasculate him with a lashing tongue. Lance is my rock and I had to learn the meaning of being a submissive wife. Not bow down to everything and allow him to dominate every aspect of my life, but to allow him to be the man God made him to be, which is head of the household. I am to support my husband, direct him when he's uncertain or off target, be his best friend, and be a productive mother to his children. Love him, care for him, and respect him. However,

being submissive doesn't mean allow him to be abusive and we all know I'm not for that.

Lance continued, "I wish there was something that I could do to reassure you that you don't have to be threatened by Sharayne."

I shook my head and said, "Honey, I'm not threatened by her. But I know a snake when I see one. Why don't you take my word on this? Why is it hard for you to understand what I'm telling you? Baby, you've told me how she dismissed you when you were together. You've told me how she rejected your marriage proposal years ago. Then the moment you move on and receive that love and dedication elsewhere, she starts to check for you. She never called you this much regarding your kids until we got married and then started calling more in a month after the twins were born. All of that is very suspect to me. But what's hurtful is that you won't even do anything about this. You brush it off."

"Okay. If you want me to stop talking to her, I will. You have my word. Plus, you were right as far as our kids calling her solely. They're old enough to communicate with her without me being involved. I guess I was just trying to stay cordial with her to show them I could still be nice to their mother though I moved on."

"For what, Lance?"

"To be honest...I don't know." Jayda fell asleep in Lance's arm so he got up and put her in her bassinette. He sat back down next to me and put his arms around me and pulled me close to him. The light blue t-shirt he wore held onto the scent of his cologne and his white jeans had streaks of blue in them that matched his shirt.

"Do me a favor?" I asked as I moved my dreadlocks off of his shirt so I could feel his chest against my face. "Don't start a debate while one of the best slow-mix CDs are playing. You messed up the groove."

Lance laughed a little. "You got it." He kissed me on my forehead and I wrapped my arms around him the best I could on the couch.

Logan and her daughters were walking down the hallway with Chantel right behind them. Amira had on a purple tank top, jean shorts, and purple sandals. She was holding Aleasha's hand and had her Bratz overnight bag over one shoulder. Aleasha was pulling her princess overnight bag with her. She was wearing jean capris and an orange t-shirt with white sandals. It was just amazing to see these two girls, who are sisters, walk hand in hand and look nothing alike. The only features that stood out that connected them to Logan were their noses and ears.
"Okay, lovebirds," Logan began, "we're headed out."
I stood up to hug and kiss my nieces and thank Logan again for staying over.
"Thank you so much, Cookie," I said.
"Anytime. Just think about what I said, okay?"
I sighed, "Yeah. I'll think it over. Drive safely and hug Brian and the boys for me."
"I will. Bye, Lance!"
Lance walked over to the front door to hug Amira and Aleasha and Logan. "See you all later," he said.
We stood at the front door and watched them get into Logan's blue Chrysler Pacifica. As they backed out of the front driveway, Lance closed the door.
"So...what does Logan want you to think about?"
I hesitated, "Huh? Oh...she, uh, told me that our grandmother may need us to visit her for a while." I walked into the kitchen to get some water and Lance followed.
"Which grandmother?" he asked.
"Grandmama," I responded.
"What's going on with her?"

"I don't know. I'm going to give her a call soon."
"Okay. Let me know if there's anything I can do."
I took a sip of water before replying, "I will."

I walked to my bedroom to shower and get into comfortable lounge-wear afterward. After putting on my favorite house clothes, I jumped into my bed, grabbed the remote, and surfed for a decent movie to look at. Then, there was a knock on the door following Chantel's entrance.
"Hey, Mo-Ma. You busy?" she asked.
"Nope," I answered. "What's up?"
She closed the door behind her then sat next to me in my bed. "I just wanna talk to see how things were with your trip."
"And what else?"
Chantel shyly smiled and looked down at her pedicured toes.
"Well...I also want your opinion on something."
I muted the television. "Sure; go for it."
"Okay, there's this guy that asked me to go with him to his senior prom. He's sooooo cute! I wanna go, but I'm afraid that Dad'll say no."
"Why do you think he'll say no?"
"Because he was in trouble before. Did three months in juvie when he was in 10th grade."
"So what has he been doing since then?"
"To my knowledge, he hasn't done anything else."
"How well do you know him?"
"Since I started my freshman year."
"Well, you know we're going to want to meet him first and then your father is going to want to have a one-on-one with him like he did Alanna's boyfriend."
"I know. I'm prepared for that. But we're not dating or anything. We're just cool."
"Girl, that doesn't matter and you know that. Shoot, he

made me spend a day with Lamar's prom date before they went."

"Oh yeah...the church girl gone bad. That was funny!"

I laughed. "Yeah. TyShanna Johnson. She had poor Lamar all twisted up in the head for a while, didn't she?"

"Mmm hmm. Even talked him into losing his virginity."

"Well, Chantel, if he was already contemplating that, she didn't have to talk him into it."

"But he said he was going to wait until marriage."

"And at the end of the day, he is still a hormonal, heterosexual male who didn't have strong enough faith and discipline to adhere to that promise. Wait...why are we talking about him and this subject? Did you do something?"

"Oh no, no, no! Not ready for that." Chantel's cell phone rang, but she ignored it. It rang again and she ignored it. It rang a third time and she became so irritated that she turned it off.

"What's wrong?" I asked.

"Why do she keep calling me?"

"Who?"

"My mother. And how did she get *this* number?"

"Oh, I'm sorry. I gave it to her this time?"

"Mo-Ma, I don't want to be bothered with her. Please don't do that again. Now I have to get my number changed."

"Why don't you wanna talked to her?"

Chantel scoot back on my bed closer to me and propped her head on her father's pillow. "She don't want to talk to me. She's always asking what's going on here in the house."

*I knew it!* I knew she was up to no good. "How long has she be quizzing you on this household?"

"For about a year. It really started after Lanni and I had been here about six months after we moved here. I don't know. She just doesn't sound genuine when she talks to me. It's always how's my relationship with you or do you ever say anything about her."

"Hmm. And you don't like that, do you?"

"No. I mean...I love her, but whenever I do go to Charlotte to visit her, she is treating me like...like...I crawled from under a rock or something. And always blamed me for her relationship with that creep falling apart."

"Well you know it wasn't your fault, right?"

"Yeah, I know."

"Good."

Lance walked in the bedroom and looked at Chantel and I. "Oh boy," he replied. "You two are having your pow-wow I see. But I need to interrupt for a while. Telly, could you excuse us for a moment?"

Chantel got up out of the bed and walked out. Lance locked the door behind him and started to undress as he walked toward the master bathroom. I don't care how agitated I get with him, I loved seeing him undress. While he was stark naked, he kept the bathroom door open and turned the shower on. He knew I was watching him and kept the show going.

"You know," he started, "it'd be nice to have some help in here."

I laughed, "I just came out of there not too long ago, Lance."

"So you're just gonna leave me hanging...literally..."

"Lance..."

He started walking toward me...completely nude. I jumped out of the bed and started for the door, but he quickly jumped in front of it.

"C'mon, now," he said rubbing his body against mine. "You denied me when we went away. Can't you tell I've been longing for you?"

I felt that familiar embrace when he was being suggestive.

"Baby, Dr. Burrell told you it was okay for us to get down

over a month ago."

I knew what she said, but I knew how I felt. I had gained thirty pounds to my once muscular 150 pound frame and still didn't lose any of the weight. I just didn't feel attractive. My stomach wasn't flat anymore, love handles were everywhere, stretch marks took over, and my thighs were huge. And here was my man standing in front of me all cut up and buff. I moved his hands off of my waist and moved back away from him with my head down.

"I can't, Lance," I said.

Holding on to my waist, he asked, "Sweetheart, what's the problem? You're not telling me something."

"Umm, can you at least wrap yourself up?"

Smiling, he said, "No."

"I'm serious."

"I am too! Okay, okay, Mo. Let me turn the shower water off. We're going to get to the bottom of this." Lance walked back to the master bathroom and turned off the shower water. He grabbed his robe from behind the door and walked to the lounge chair and sat. He opened his arms for me to sit on his lap so I did. Stroking my dreads, Lance asked, "What's going on, Mo? Seriously."

I took in a deep breath. I normally have such an easy time telling him how I was feeling that it came as a shock to me that I was feeling like a scared child admitting I did something wrong. "Lance...I...I don't feel comfortable...yet."

"Huh? What are you talking about?"

"I feel...fat...and my body's all...weird to me now."

"Are you serious?"

"Yes! Why wouldn't I be? I mean look at me! I'm damn near 200 pounds, I can't fit any of my clothes, I'm cut up, stretched out, and just..."

"...beautiful to me," Lance finished. "Morgan, you had my babies, almost lost your life, and you're worried about your figure?" Lance moved me off of his lap so I could sit next to him. "To be honest, this extra you have looks good on you. Beyond that, you're my wife. How would I look telling you to lose weight or change your physical appearance after all you've just gone through? When I vowed for better or worse, I meant that. You have to want to lose weight for yourself, not for me or anyone else. Just remember, I love you for who you are. I've gotten to know and love you unconditionally and death is the only thing that'll get rid of me; not baby fat. You understand that?"

I shook my head up and down to show I understood.

"Now...can I have some honey?" he asked.

"Sugar isn't enough?"

"Nope. My body is ailing...I'm coming down with something and I need some honey to ease the pain."

Without hesitation, my husband leaned in to me and kissed me gently and deeply. I felt his strong hands pull me under him and the only thing I could do was submit.

\*\*\*\*\*\*\*\*\*\*\*\*\*\*\*\*\*\*\*\*\*\*\*\*\*\*\*\*\*\*\*\*\*\*\*\*\*\*\*\*\*\*\*\*\*\*\*\*\*\*\*\*

The next day, I went to work. It was the second week upon my returning from maternity leave and there was a lot I had to get caught up on, though Joanne Bell took on my cases as my backup. I checked dozens of emails, voicemails, and postal mail that could not have been handled by my backup nor through Mrs. Lopez. After about an hour and a half of responding back to the senders, I came across an envelope that almost made me jump out of my skin from excitement. My college buddy Autumn Reyes sent me a letter and I opened it with excitement.

*"Hey, Morgan!*

*I heard through the grapevine that you were married with children now and I'll be honest when I say I couldn't believe it!*

*Let me send my congrats to you and that lucky man who managed to tame you. I honestly thought you would never get married after all you went through to try and salvage your relationship with Thomas and that fiasco with Jerome, but I'm glad that you were able to get pass all of that to allow happiness to come in. Even that short arrangement you had with Victor your senior year at IUP made me believe you'd never allow a man to try to win your heart.*

*I recently got back from London and it was an experience I'll never forget! The sights, the people, the culture… I could go on and on. I've been contemplating on moving there, but I don't think I'll be able to do so without a familiar face or two.*

*Anyway, I'll be in the Atlanta area the last week of August and I have to come see you and your husband. Since you're unlisted in the phone directories, I figured I'd reach out and contact you at your job; I hope I wasn't out of line for this. Call me when you get this letter. My number is 215-999-9999.*

*Take care and talk to you soon!*

*Much love,*

*Autumn*

Oh…my…goodness! Victor!

## Chapter Three

On the way home from work, I called Logan. I had to have a pow-wow with her face to face. After that letter from Autumn, it sparked a part of my past I didn't want to remember. However, I felt that it was connected to that crazy dream I had shortly after I fell into that short coma. While I drove to her house, I tried to remember more of my dealings with him. Victor Diez was a young man of Cuban and Italian descent. He was very charming, intelligent, and so handsome that I was shocked he showed me the time of day in our English Composition courses. He stood at five foot eight (slightly shorter than me), had thick, jet black hair, a neatly trimmed goatee, and icy blue eyes. He always dressed neatly and seemed borderline metrosexual. His teeth were so straight and white that when he smiled he lit up a room. His skin tone was like no other I've ever seen and it didn't display any sign of blemishes. Victor...a man I wanted to forget.

\*\*\*\*\*\*\*\*\*\*\*\*\*\*\*\*\*\*\*\*\*\*\*\*\*\*\*\*\*\*\*\*\*\*\*\*\*\*\*\*\*\*\*\*\*\*\*\*\*\*\*\*\*\*\*

It was the beginning of the fall semester 1998. I sat in the back row of the English Composition 401 class taking notes and trying to keep up with the professor's lecture. I was so engulfed in writing that I didn't know someone was asking me for the time.

"Excuse me," a male's voice said, "do you have the time?" Without looking at him, I looked at my watch and said, "9:25."

"Thank you," the guy said. Seconds later, "Excuse me, again. I hate to bother you, but—"

"—Well, why do you keep..." I stopped myself from continuing my thought once I looked up at the face where the voice came from. The thought that came to me was *damn!* Then I asked, "What can I help you with?"

With a smile, the young man said, "I'm sorry. My name is Victor and I just transferred into this class last week. Do you have any notes I can borrow? You seem to be on point with what's going on in here."

"How can you determine if I'm on point or not?" I asked.

"Unless you're just bullshittin', your notebook looks pretty full from what I can see."

"So, you just sit next to folks and look over their shoulders?"

"Naw. Well, okay, maybe I do sometimes. I usually don't do this though."

I hesitated but those eyes just did me in and I couldn't say no. I pulled the rings back on my binder and pulled out a couple of sheets of notes to share with him and handed them to him. With a smile, Victor said, "Thanks. I promise I'll give them back."

"Sure," I answered.

After class was over, I grabbed my things and walked out heading to my last class of the morning. I was almost out of the corridor when I felt a tap on my shoulder. I turned around and saw Victor handing me my notes.

"I appreciate it," he declared.

Taking my notes back, I said, "You're welcome." I continued to walk toward the building's exit when I heard, "Yo! Hold up...what's your name?" Next thing I knew, Victor was walking in stride next to me. Without missing a step, I answered, "Morgan."

"Nice," Victor said.

"What's so nice about that?" I questioned.

"I've always liked that name for a girl," he answered.

"Where are you on your way to?"

"My next class," I replied.

"Well, can I see you sometime later to go over some things for this class?" he asked.

"I suppose that wouldn't be a bad idea," I said. "Sure." Meet me at the library at 3 this afternoon if you can."

"I can do that. Thank you, Miss Morgan," Victor said with a smile.

"You're welcome, Mister Victor," I said. As I walked to my next class, I felt like I was 12 years old all over again when I first met Kevin Littleton. I was just hoping I didn't come off too corny because deep down, I was instantly attracted to Victor's appearance.

I ran into my new roommate, Patrice, when I was on my way to the library. She had just come from her part-time daylight job at the corner store down the street from campus still in her uniform.

"What's going on, Mo?!" Patrice greeted in her effervescent voice.

"Done with classes...about to go to the library," I replied.

"I should plan on getting there some time this evening myself. I have to start compiling information for my journal research assignment. How long are you going to be there?" she asked.

"Not sure," I answered. "I'm meeting someone to go over some notes in English comp."

"Really? Who?"

"Some new guy in my class. Name's Victor."

"What year is he?"

"I'm guessing he's a senior too. I didn't ask."

"What does he look like? I know a guy named Victor."

"Tell me who you *don't* know!" I burst out laughing.

"Well, you know me...the social butterfly."

"Mmm hmm. The nosy butterfly. Well, he's a little shorter than I am, he's definitely not a black guy—"

"—light blue eyes, dark hair, smells good, and dresses nice?"

"Damn, Patrice! Yeah...that's him."

"Giiiirrrrrlllll!!!! That's Victor Diez! Do you have any idea how many females try to get at him and get their feelings hurt?"
"What are you talking about?"
"Morgan, Victor was voted Homecoming King since he started here as a freshman. Remember...him and Autumn were Homecoming King and Queen the fall of '97?"
"Oh, yeah! I remember her telling me about that. She was so happy that she was paired up her senior year in court with that dude because, as she put it, their pictures were going to turn out good! He looks different this year."
Patrice nodded her head, "Yup. That's because he's a little more buff and let that facial hair grow in. For a while, he was kinda skinny."
"The facial hair," I agreed. "That's why he looks different. He didn't have it when he took that homecoming picture."
"Well," Patrice said as she was walking to our apartment building, "I'm going to go shower and change. I would say I'll meet up with you, but I don't want to impose."
"Trice, come down if you want. Ain't nobody hooking up for a date or anything," I stated.
"Oh yeah...you have a boyfriend who you only see during summer vacation back in Pittsburgh," she countered. "I'll catch you later."
"Alright," I said.

As I walked to the library with my materials, I heard a familiar voice beckon my name. I turned around to see Victor with a backpack jogging toward me. He had on a green button down shirt and black jeans and all white sneakers. It was like I was looking at a movie star and I was trying my best not to gawk at him. There's got to be something about him that would be surface negatively because no one that handsome could float around on campus and not be taken.

"Hey," I said, "you're kinda early."

As he stopped jogging and began to walk, he said, "I was going to grab some coffee from the café before I met you. But since I saw you walking in, I thought I'd ask if you wanted something too and I'll bring it to you."

"I don't drink coffee," I stated.

"They have other drinks. Soda, or as you Pittsburghers call it, pop...they also have cocoa, water..." Victor implied.

"I'll just take some bottled water."

"Alright...done. I'll meet you inside. Where are you going to be sitting?"

"Look for me," I said slyly.

With that bright, killer smile, Victor said, "Alright. See you in a bit."

I walked inside and found a table next to the computer stations. The carpeted library smelled like mildewed paper. I sat my backpack down in a chair to reserve a spot for Victor and I pulled my books and notebooks out of it. The pink jogging suit I had on was holding onto some of the sweat off of my body that secreted due to the late summer heat. I just hoped that I didn't smell like sweat. It would've left a bad impression for my first study session. Then I thought why should I care? I was dating Thomas. Then again who was I kidding? I knew Thomas was doing his own thing though he wouldn't admit it. But after a bad fiasco with my former college buddy Jerome, I was hesitant on doing anything with anyone no matter how they approached me.

"Here's your water, Morgan," Victor announced startling me a little.

"Oh...you scared me! Thanks though," I replied.

Victor sat down across from me and pulled his materials out of his backpack. Then he asked, "So what's Professor Donnelly like? Does he seem like a stickler or an instructor willing to work with his students?"

"It's only been a week," I answered. "I haven't felt him out yet. In all honesty, I don't really care about any of the professors' personalities. I just want to get my work and do the best I can so I can get on with my life."

"Really?" Victor inquired. "Don't you think it's important to know what kind of person you're working with?"

"What do you mean?"

"Well, you know...think of it as he's your supervisor. You wouldn't just want to show up and not know if he was anal retentive and a stickler for rules, would you?"

"I see what you're saying," I said. "But I don't work and I've never had an after school job when I was in high school, so that's a little unfamiliar to me."

Victor raised his eyebrows and said, "Seriously? You never worked...ever?"

"Nope."

"How do you manage what you do here? Student loans...grants...?"

"Scholarships. Don't you think you're getting kind of personal asking me about my financial status?"

"Oh, I'm sorry. I don't mean to intrude. I was just trying to break the ice. So what's your major?"

"Elementary education. Yours?"

"Forensic law. I'm going to get my master's elsewhere. I can't take the north anymore."

"Hmm. You're going to be in school for a while, I see."

"Oh and you're not?"

"Nope. Not until I'm ready to get my master's. I already have my student-teacher assignment set up to start next week at one of the Indiana County elementary schools which will meet my requirements to earn my degree for the Spring. I stuck to my plan and I'm about to be outta here. Four years is enough."

"Impressive. Congratulations."

"Thank you. Now...what do you need for this class so you can catch up?"

Victor pulled out his syllabus and checked off some of the assignments he needed to turn in to get caught up. We spent the next forty-five minutes going over the objectives, what the professor was looking for, and studied the vocabulary. The butterflies went away once we got entrenched in the work and I forgot how attractive he was for the last thirty minutes of working together. We spent a total of two hours in the library working, researching, and of course...talking.

When I recognized it was 5 o'clock, I started to gather my things. My stomach was growling and I had to get something to eat.

"Well, this was nice," I said. "But I gotta go. I'm hungry and have some things to do before tomorrow."

Victor stood up, "Wait a minute. Take this." He handed me a folded piece of paper. "This is my address and phone number. Call me later or come by."

"Come by? Dude...we just met today. I'm not going to your place."

"Ouch!" he replied. "I've never been shot down like that before."

As I put the strap of my backpack over my right shoulder and pushed my chair in, I said, "Victor, you seem like a nice guy and I know you know you look good and probably have any woman you want by flashing that handsome set of pearly whites. But one thing you have to understand about me is that though I like to look at a good looking man, I don't get buckled like your average female. I'll call you later."

Victor stood and shook his head. "Okay, Mami. Looking forward to it."

I walked out of the library and headed to my student apartment building. I put my headphones on and started my CD walkman and listened to my R. Kelly CD as I walked. If that was Logan, she would've jumped all over that guy.

At the end of the fall semester, I was packing to go back to Pittsburgh for Winter break. Since I was returning in January, I didn't take need to take everything with me. Patrice had already left the day before and I enjoyed having the apartment to myself. Don't get me wrong now. Patrice was a sweetheart, but she was a heavy weed smoker and I was so glad I wasn't getting a contact off of the residue that is normally floating in the air by the time I got up in the morning. She was very thin and was dark skinned. She was into the 70s style and kept her hair in this really pretty afro that was accentuated with some type of hair accessory; like a headband or scarf that matched her earrings. One thing I could say about her was if she was your friend, then she was ride or die. She spoke what was on her mind even if it was offensive to others and there were times when she her remarks caused crazy altercations with some of the girls on campus. However, one thing that I learned about her during our junior year was that she was bisexual and I found that out by a very uncomfortable arrival to our apartment and found her in bed with her boyfriend and her girlfriend because she left her bedroom door open. That's right; she was dating both and they were all open and accepting of it. Anyway, just as I was finished throwing out perishable food in the refrigerator, the phone rang. I walked over to the counter where the telephone sat and picked it up.
"Hello?" I answered.
"Good...you're there," the voice on the other end said. It was Victor. "I wanted to drop something off to you before you left. Can I come by?"

"What is it?" I asked.

"The Ginuwine CD you let me borrow," he answered.

"Man, that could've waited. But okay," I said.

"Cool. I'll be there in about ten minutes."

We hung up and I went back to packing and cleaning. A lot had happened between Victor and I since we first met. He got me into this business with him that I shouldn't have gotten involved with, but my inheritance money wouldn't kick in until I graduated in the spring and the allotment I usually received from Grandmama wasn't coming anymore. Logan would send me some money from Charlotte when she could and my cousin Courtney helped out too. I know I should've just found a job, but Grandmama told me not to worry about anything and I always trusted what she told me. But I needed money and I couldn't wait on the inheritance money from my grandfather Willie James to fall. So during one of our study sessions I shared some of my personal business with Victor and he helped me earn some money.

A knock on my apartment door came in the timeframe that was given. I didn't have to look through the peephole because I knew Victor was going to be on the other side. Dressed in a dark green Nike sweat suit, he entered my apartment and closed the door behind him. He glanced around the living room and said, "All set, huh?"

"Yup," I replied. "Just gotta take my stuff down once my cousin comes pick me up."

"How long's it gonna be before he gets here?" Victor asked.

"Not for at least another two hours," I said. Courtney always came at the same time every end of semester; 5 o'clock.

"Well, here's your CD. Thanks for letting me use it. It was alright."

"I'm just shocked that you never heard it. It's been out for over a year."

"Well, I'm not really into rap and R&B all like that. I mean some of it's cool, but I'm into jazz and of course that Latin flavor. Oh before I forget, here." He handed me an unmarked white envelope. "Merry Christmas. I hope this comes in handy."

"What's this for?" I asked. "You already paid me."

"Consider it a bonus. You're the only woman who I can say is about that money when it's all said and done. I earned a lot of business because of you."

"Thank you, Victor," I said taking the envelope from him.

"Sure. Um, Morgan?"

"What's up?"

"I know you have your main guy and all that, but I don't think it's going to work out with me being your man on campus only."

"What are you talking about?"

"Morgan...I've fallen for you; hard. And I'm doing all I can to keep from losing my composure over this arrangement we have."

"Victor, I can't—"

"You can't what? Leave a dude that's doing himself just like you're doing you right now? Do you have any idea what it's like for me knowing that you're going to spend your time at home with this other guy?"

"C'mon, man! You said you'd be okay with this!"

"Damn, that was before now!" He walked closer to me and put his hands on my shoulders. "Morgan, I don't like when you leave in the middle of the night to come back here after we do our thing and I hate when you take that dude's calls when we're together. I want to see you over the winter break at some point and to be honest...I want you to stop seeing that dude. I want to be the *only* man in your life; not the side dick."

"Vic, I can't. I mean...I have love for him; I still love him."
"Morgan, that's bullshit and you know it! If you loved him like you say you do, then you wouldn't be loving me. Or are you doing this with me because you can't do this with him?" He dropped his hands and leaned against my kitchen wall. "You mean to tell me you're still in love with some lame, high school relationship? You don't want to move on and enjoy what's in front of you?"
"Why are you doing this to me? Huh? Why?"
I turned to walk toward the door and he grabbed my arm aggressively.
"Me doing to you?! How about you playing with my heart?! How about I'm rejecting all types of fuzz because you got me open? I've had girls come at me for a long time and I used them to my disposal for years. But I've never had a girl come into my life like you. You're smart, beautiful, erotic as hell, and you have a drive for life."
"Let go of me, Victor!" I said snatching away from him. But he grabbed my arm again but with extreme force.
"Stop pulling away from me, Morgan!" he demanded as he grabbed me by both of my arms. My very skinny arms were locked in Victor's grip. He pulled me closer to him and angrily kissed me. I bit his tongue until he let me go and then I saw his open hand come down and connect with my face. In a rage, I began punching him in the face. He was so stunned that he backed up and for the first time, I saw a demonic look in those icy blue eyes of his. He charged me to the floor and straddled me where I couldn't move. He slapped me in the face two more times and began choking me. I managed to swing my legs up to get them around his neck and flipped him off of me. But as I tried to get up, he grabbed the top of my pants and pulled me back to the floor. With one hand on my neck pinning me to the floor, he used his other hand to continue to pull my pants down

below my waist. His knees and legs pinned my thighs down on the floor and before I knew it, this guy was raping me. The more I yelled for him to stop, the more he continued. This was not the same guy I thought I knew. Every night I spent with him was now marred with this unforgiving and despicable act of hate. And little did he know, vengeance was going to be mine.

After he came, his body slumped on mine like he normally did. He was still breathing heavily and I felt the sweat of his forehead drip on the back of my neck. I was so pissed that I couldn't cry. I couldn't do anything. He finally got off of me and stood up. He had the audacity to pull my pants up over my waist before he whispered in my ear, "I love you, Morgan. I hope you're not mad...but if you are, I'm sorry." He kissed my cheek then walked out the door. I stayed on that floor in complete horror. Lying there trying to understand what just happened. All I knew at that point was I wasn't going to call the police; I was going to kill that dude or at least make him wish he were dead.

I took another shower and changed my clothes before Courtney arrived. The clothes I had on were thrown in a trash bag because they reeked of evil. I sat and waited for Courtney to come pick me up and replayed over and over again what had just happened. Did I bring that on myself? Why didn't I just break it off completely with Thomas? What was I trying to prove by keeping that relationship? Then, it hit me...no matter what I had done I didn't deserve to get assaulted and raped. So I picked up my switchblade and ran out of my apartment door and headed over to Victor's. With long strides, I got to his apartment building within five minutes. I saw him standing in front of his door unlocking it and as soon he opened it to enter, I charged him with the blade going in and out of his back repetitively. He screamed in agony and fell to the floor. I slammed the door behind us. He turned over to find me standing over him. Quickly, I stomped his genitals with my Timberland boots. When he seized for his groin, with all I had, I kicked him in the jaw as if his head were a kickball. "You like to rape motherfuckers, don't you?!" I yelled with another stomp to the face. I was about to do it again, but he caught my ankle and deflected the impact. I lost my balance, but didn't fall. Victor tried to get up, but the stabs in the back kept him grounded.

"I didn't rape you!" he yelled.

"Bitch, I didn't consent!" I yelled back and with one last swing to the face with my blade, I sliced his face from the right temple to the corner of his bottom lip.

"Ahhh!" he screamed.

"And I got your DNA all in me and on my clothes along with the bruises on my body! You try to press charges on me, Mr. Forensic Law Student, and I'll pull out my trump card for self-defense!"

I walked out of his apartment and out of the building. There was an audience in the lobby of the building and I didn't entertain any of the stares or questions. With streaks and spots of Victor's blood on me, I ran back to my apartment and waited for Courtney to take me home.

\*\*\*\*\*\*\*\*\*\*\*\*\*\*\*\*\*\*\*\*\*\*\*\*\*\*\*\*\*\*\*\*\*\*\*\*\*\*\*\*\*\*\*\*\*\*\*\*\*\*\*

I arrived at Logan's house an hour after I got off from work. Her front yard had a flower bed that was full of beautiful yellow and red roses. On the side of the house were bikes and toys that belonged to Austin and Aleasha. I parked my Durango next to her silver Pathfinder in the driveway. As I walked up to the front door, I heard a bunch of commotion which was normal. I rang the bell and waited for someone to open it. Standing before me was Brian on the other side with a big smile on his face.

"Hey, Mo," he greeted. "C'mon in." He stepped aside so I could enter and closed the door behind me.

"How are you?" I asked giving him a hug.

"I'm good. Trying to get used to my new aids. They're a lot clearer than the other ones I had and I can hear almost everything now. Since Janelle and Amira want to practice being fully hearing, I thought we'd try not to sign this week."

"Brian, that's a little odd," I added. "It's not like nobody in this house can sign."

"It's an experiment. Only for two days. Janelle said that it's better to be deaf and Amira said it's better to be hearing. A.J. said it's better to be hearing and able to sign. I said let's put it to a test. So, whatever you do, don't...sign."

I laughed, "Okay! Where's Logan?"

"In the den."

I walked from the threshold to the back of the house where the den was set up. Logan was sitting at her desk with a lot of papers in front of her. She looked up and recognized I was walking in and stood up. "Hey, Mo!"

"Hey, Cookie. What're you doing?"

"Getting caught up with all of this paperwork from my job. I have to do a presentation in two days on effective ways to be cost effective."

"Hmm. Sounds like fun," I said as I sat down on the oversized sofa.

Logan walked over and sat next to me, "So...what's up?"

"Do you remember that whole incident that happened to me with Victor?"

"That creep?! Yeah I remember! I still don't understand why you didn't press charges!"

"Well, you remember when I told you about that dream or premonition I had when I was having the twins?"

"Yeah, I remember."

"Well, I got a letter from Autumn some time ago and she mentioned him."

"Okay..."

"And remember I told you what the guy said to me in that dream?"

"Mmm hmm."

"Cookie, Victor was the guy in my dream."

"Huh?! How?!"

"I worked for him that semester before things went south with me and him."

"Doing what?!"

I took a deep breath and started to spill my guts. "Victor ran a company that serviced prominent men in the county with call girls, escorts, and prostitutes. I was like a madam, but I never went out and slept with anyone that was seeking company."

Logan's mouth dropped and she leaned back in the couch. She gave me a look that was so unfamiliar to me. Next thing I know, she slapped me. In total shock, I stood up and found her nose to nose with me.

"What the fuck, Logan?!" I yelled.

"How could you?! Why did you do that?! Of all of the stupid shit you've done, you did *that?!*"

"First of all, how the hell you gonna slap me and think I'm not contemplating beating your ass in your house?! That was a long time ago, Logan!"

"But those women you solicited...like they were toys! Like they weren't shit! You were no different than some of the men in our family...only out for Morgan!"

"Don't you think I know that now?!"

Logan walked away from me and gazed out the window. Without looking at me, she asked, "You remember Imani Jones? The girl I became friends with our freshman year with after that whole Gerald and Autumn incident from the frat party?"

"No."

"Oh, you don't?" she questioned as she turned to look at me. Her thick arms flexed through her powder blue tank top and her hands rested sternly on hips. "Let me refresh your memory. Imani was about five two, brown skin, had a tattoo of a dragon going up and down her left arm with the name Blaze over it. She usually had her hair styled like Aaliyah's." The more Logan described her friend, the more I started to remember. The more I remembered, the more I felt a lump in my throat. Her friend was only referred to as Blaze. I never knew her name. She was one of Victor's girls and was a very high earner.

"Oh, yeah, you know who I'm talking about. The expression on your face says everything, Mo!"

"Logan…"

"Well because of *you* and *Victor* my friend, the only other female I'd refer to as a sister, was damn near beat to death by a lunatic asshole her senior year because she didn't want to take it up the ass! My friend lied in that hospital bed for two weeks with injuries she was going to have to live with for the rest of her life. When she called me in Charlotte and told me what happened, I was crushed. I remember asking her time and time again to tell me how she got involved with that line of work, but she would never tell me. She *knew* you were my sister and she *trusted* you! That's why she never told me how she got into that job; because you were involved!"

"Logan, I'm sorry about what happened to her. To be honest, there's a lot of that time of my life I suppressed and—"

"—cut the shit, Morgan! You have an excuse for everything reckless you've ever done! But because you're my sister, I've excused a lot! When are you going to start owning up and fix the shit you've caused?!"

Brian walked into the den. With a confused look on his face, he asked, "What's going on in here? A.J. can hear you two arguing."

"Brian, honey, not right now," Logan answered agitatedly. Without a debate, he walked out and closed the door behind him.

"Logan, I didn't have anything to do with Blaze...Imani...getting into that life. She was doing that before I got on board. When Victor introduced me to everyone, she asked me not to tell you because she felt embarrassed and wanted to tell you on her own. She adored you, Logan, and didn't want you to see her any differently. I was the one who told her to let you know what was going on with her because I knew how much your friendship meant the world to you." I walked over to Logan and sucker-punched her so hard she fell out on the floor. "But for as long as you live, you better not ever...*EVER*...put your hands on me!" She held her face and looked up at me and hurriedly got up on her feet. In my defense stance, I said, "You sure you wanna do this, Cookie?!"

"Mo, you know I have never been afraid of you! But you're not gonna disrespect me in my house!"

"You're coming at me over your friend?"

"No!"

"Then what the hell are you doing?!"

"I don't know!" Logan walked away from me with her hands up as if she was throwing me away. "You need some serious psychological help, Mo."

"And I love you too," I sarcastically stated. I walked toward my sister and said, "I'm sorry for keeping that secret from you."

Logan still had her hands on her hips. With a very stern look, she said, "I love you too, Morgan. But your past is scary as hell and it's starting to affect my life." I pulled her close to me to give her a hug. After we embraced and apologized, I sat back down on the couch.

"So when is Autumn coming into town?" Logan inquired.

"Probably sometime next week," I answered.

"It'd be good to see her."

"Yeah," I agreed. "It's been about seven years since I've seen her. Two years since we last talked."

"Morgan, what really happened with you and Victor?"

"Huh? What do you mean?"

"See...I know you only dish out what you feel is necessary; even with me. And I know you never told Autumn what happened with you two."

"I've told you everything that happened with us, Logan."

"So because you rejected being exclusive, he went into a rage and raped you?"

"Yes! What more do you want from that?!"

"I'm just checking. But you were treading on thin ice anyway dealing with him."

"Why?"

"Hello? His father was Cuban and his mother was Italian. That's a volatile mixture of nuts, if you ask me. I don't give a shit how cute someone is, and he was fine, I still couldn't have gotten with him."

Brian walked in again, this time looking at both of us like we were crazy.

"What's with the hand print on your face, Mo? And the cut lip on you, Logan? What the hell's going on in here??!"

"Nothing, baby," Logan said walking to him. "We just had a disagreement, but we're cool now."

Brian looked at me...hard. He didn't blink nor take his gaze off of me and to be honest, it sent a chill down my spine. Putting his arm around Logan, he said to me, "It's been nice, Morgan, but it's time for you to go home."

Baffled, I asked, "You're kicking me out?"

"If someone puts their hands on my wife, in my house, they're going to have a bad day. Now we don't want to go there, do we?"

"Baby, we're cool. We made up," Logan pleaded.

"It's cool, Sis. It's time for me to go anyway. I'm pretty sure Alanna is tired of babysitting," I said. As I walked out of the den, Brian was right behind me and Logan behind him.

"Morgan, I'll call you," Logan said as I walked out of the door. I felt awful because I couldn't even tell my nieces and nephews goodnight. Brian slammed the door closed no sooner than both of my feet were out of their house. I was so ashamed and so hurt by what just happened that tears welled up and streamed down my face as I walked to my truck.

I arrived home to find Alanna doing homework with Chantel keeping an eye on the babies. I felt bad and I guess it was obvious because Alanna looked up and ran over to me.

"Mo-Ma, what's wrong?" she asked.

"Nothing; just tired," I lied.

Her ballerina body standing at five feet six hugged me. She had her hair pulled up in a bun and was dressed in a white velour pantsuit. Her dark brown eyes was outlined with black eyeliner and the little diamond stud in her nose sparkled.

"You hungry? Dad said it was cool to just order pizza today."

"Pizza would be good," I said putting my keys on the key rack by the living room entrance.

"Oh, Aunt Lo called. She said to call her once you got in since you didn't pick up your cell," Alanna stated as she went back to the dining room table to do her homework.

"Thank you," I said. I walked to the living room and picked

up Jayda to give her a kiss. Jayden noticed me and started kicking his little legs rapidly. Once I got my kisses with Jayda, I picked up her brother and sat down holding both of them on the couch. I looked at these two babies and smiled. No matter how my day ended, I was more relaxed smelling and holding them. I heard the house phone ring, but I didn't want to answer it. Then, Chantel walked in with the phone. Handing it to me, she said, "It's Aunt Lo."

"Tell her I'll call her back," I replied.

"Aunt Lo, she has the babies and will call you back," Chantel spoke into the receiver. One thing I loved about her was that she could pick up and run with anything with minimal direction. As she walked down the hall to her room, the side door opened and in walked Lance in his GBI uniform.

"Hey, baby," he said walking to me and picking up Jayda from my lap. "How was your day?"

"Where should I begin?" I inquired.

"Damn, was it that bad?" he asked.

"No...work was fine. It was the visit to Logan's house that tripped up the evening."

"What did you go over there for? Why do you have a handprint on the side of your face? Mo, what did you do to her?"

I didn't want to tell him what happened out in the open, so he followed me to our bedroom. Once in there, I told everything that had happened at Logan's house to Lance at that moment. Every...thing. Even about the dream that he wasn't aware of. Needless to say, Lance was shocked when he learned of my dealings with Victor and even more caught off guard that Logan and I assaulted each other. While bouncing Jayda on his knee, he looked at me squinting his eyes.

"Morgan Brooks," he began, "what all do I need to know about you that I wasn't able to pull up on a background check I did on you a year ago?"

"You did a background check on me?"

"Yes! Why wouldn't I? Your sister killed my brother, you shot your ex-boyfriend Kevin, and then you blackmailed Kevin and his girlfriend Quiana. Now you're telling me that you were involved with some call girl or escort service when you were in college? What else do I need to know that you haven't told me, Morgan? Right here, right now...tell me everything you've ever done that was reckless. This is your only chance to come clean with me."

That night, for the first time ever, I unleashed my Pandora's Box and told Lance everything about my past.

I told him about every person I hurt, every ruthless act I've committed, and every pain I'd inflicted upon others who I felt hurt me. I told him about my childhood and I told him about my family. That night was the first night I'd ever see Lance emotional. I've seen him angry and disappointed, but never sad or frustrated or empathetically affected by my story. When I finished talking and answering his questions, he took a shower. I didn't know how to take the silence. It was very unusual and uneasy. I took that quiet time to feed and bathe Jayden. After getting him settled, my phone rang. It was Grandmama.

"Hey, Gal," that strong, southern voice came through the receiver.

"Hi, Grandmama," I said trying not to let my voice quiver. "How are you?"

"Oh, I'm fine, Gal. How are those babies?"

"Good. I just got Jayden settled for the night. Jayda is nowhere near tired."

"Ha, ha, ha. I betcha she like her Mama. Listen, Gal, I need ta ask you a question. Now, I know you just got back to work and all, but I wanna know if y'all can come up this way here for our family reunion next year."

"Umm, I don't know."

"It's not until next July. Y'all have plenty of time."

"I honestly don't know, Grandmama. I probably could---"

"No...not just you...all of y'all. Well, I haven't seen y'all and I wanna see those babies and that fine husband of yours. Ya know I only seen him twice since you and Prissy killed his brother."

I chuckled. She had a way with words. "I'll see what we can do, Grandmama. I miss you a lot."

"Mmm. If ya did, ya would be up here more ta see me."

"Or you could just come down here and visit. I'm pretty sure your sister would be happy to see you."

"Mmm...well...I don't know...maybe. Kiss everyone for me. Love you."

"Love you, too. Goodnight."

"That was your grandmother?" Lance asked startling me.

"Damn, you scared me! Yes, it was her."

"How is she?"

"She's good and wants us to go visit."

"I see. When?"

"Whenever we can."

"Well...arrange something with your job. We're going up there."

"Huh? Why?"

"Because there's some things about you that I need to know for myself that discussion alone won't remedy for me."

"Now you're being silly," I remarked. "I don't believe you expect for me to just drop everything because you wanna investigate my life. We'll go...but not right away."

Walking toward me, Lance put his arms around my waist. "Mo, you came into my life through a tragedy. I don't wanna lose you to tragedy. I feel like you're hiding something from me about you; something more than what you've shared."

"How can you tell me this?" I asked pushing him away. "Were my confessions not viable enough for you?"

"No...baby...you're missing what I'm saying. Yes, you've told me about your past and why you did what you did, but I need to know *who* and *what* caused you so much pain in your life that you decided to carry it with you."

"Lance, I'm not carrying anything with me now."

"That may be true, but what just happened when you talked to Autumn and your sister? Another one of your skeletons rose from the dead. Mo...I have to see and feel where you came from."

"This sounds like a bunch of shit to me, but okay."

"Are you that embarrassed of your family?"

Sitting down on our lounge, I confessed, "Yes...I am."

"Girl, all families have issues, secrets, and scandals. But I love you. All of you. As long as we continue to have open communication, honesty, trust, and be upfront with each other, nothing can come between us."

Lance leaned over and kissed me on my forehead. "As far as that whole thing with you and your sister in college, you need to do something to remedy that. I don't like how Brian handled you, but I understand where he's coming from."

Lance walked out of our bedroom and closed the door behind him. I looked out of our bedroom window and gazed at the gray clouds that looked as if they were brewing for a storm. I hated the idea of going to Pittsburgh; even for a family reunion. Don't get me wrong, I love my family and some people I've known throughout high school, but I couldn't shake the bad memories. How could I go without getting emotional? A knock was on my bedroom door so I got up and walked over to it. I opened it and Chantel was standing there.

"Mo-Ma, is it okay to talk?" the curvy, young girl asked.

"Sure! C'mon in," I said allowing her to walk in. Jayden and

Jayda were sleeping in their stow-away next to my bed. Chantel walked over and sat down on the lounge and I sat at the foot of my bed to face her. "Mo-Ma, remember we were talking about that boy I wanna go to the prom with?" Smiling, I said, "Yes, what about him?"

"Well, he asked me to date him," Chantel replied.

"Okay...what's the problem? You obviously like him," I remarked.

"I know, but, it's my brother Keenan and Dad. They're not going to be with it."

"Chantel, you're 15 years old, very smart and savvy, and extremely responsible. I'm pretty sure you can handle what will come your way. If you really like him and he's taken an interest to you as well, then give it a try. Just lay down the rules and standards on what you expect from him. If he doesn't respect you enough on the standards you set for yourself, then you don't need to waste your time."

Smiling, Chantel said, "I know...and I will. Thank you!" She sprung up off of the couch and walked out of my room. While the babies were sleeping, I decided to lie down as well to take a nap.

\*\*\*\*\*\*\*\*\*\*\*\*\*\*\*\*\*\*\*\*\*\*\*\*\*\*\*\*\*\*\*\*\*\*\*\*\*\*\*\*\*\*\*\*\*\*\*\*\*\*\*\*\*\*

April 1983. Logan and I were visiting our Uncle Sambo over in Carrick. He wasn't our real uncle, but considering our mom moved on and got into a relationship with our little brother Joseph's father, Daniel, we were asked to refer to them as our new family. Our mother was sitting in the dining room talking to Daniel's family while Logan and I were playing with some of the kids who were there. They were still trying to grasp the concept that we weren't twins but were the same age. I tried to explain it was only for another month until I was going to turn 6, but trying to get a bunch of kids to understand what I was saying was hard.

Anyway, Uncle Sambo and his wife lived in a huge, yellow brick house on Brownsville Road. They had three sons who were all older than we were, but the middle son, Teddy, seemed to have a lot of interest in me and Logan. He was ten years old and his skin was almost a golden brown color, had curly jet black hair, and dark brown eyes surrounded by thick eyelashes. It was a mild day during the spring season so we all went into the backyard to play. There had to be at least a total of 14 kids outside playing different games. Some of the boys played football, some of the girls played with dolls, and some of the boys and girls played together. Then we all decided to play hide and seek. That was the idea of one of Uncle Sambo's older nieces, Syreena. I wanted to be like her so bad I could spit. She was gorgeous! She was around 12 years old, green eyes, straight brown hair that was down her back, and had this aura about her that demanding attention and respect. She was a tomboy who was "that girl" that every boy wanted. You know...the cute girl that could hang with the guys, whoop some ass, and still showed her femininity. I knew I'd never have green eyes, but she became the girl I looked up to. Anyway, Teddy was found by Syreena and she tagged him it. He went to the garage door, which was our home base, and began to count. Logan and I ran around to find a hiding place. Whenever we played a game like this with other kids, we'd hide together or not too far from one another. This time, she took off and hid behind a tree and I went over to the next yard of an empty house and hid on the side of it close enough to an unmaintained shrub that grew uncontrollably. It was so thick, no one could see through it so it was perfect. I kept peeking through making sure I didn't move. My blue jean cut off shorts and white t-shirt was so dirty I probably was like camouflage. Or so I thought. I was so busy peering through the shrubbery that I didn't even feel

Teddy behind me. But what started as fun quickly turned to horror for me. I started to run, thinking I could outrun him. He tripped me and I fell hard onto the grass. I was about to cry, but he quickly picked me up and carried me to the other side of the empty house where nobody could see us. He said, "Let me see where it's hurts."

I pointed to my knee where a huge scrape appeared with blood seeping from it.

"I'm gonna make it feel better. Just don't tell our secret, okay?" Teddy said.

"Okay," I agreed. As a five year old, you automatically assume that your boo-boos are cleaned, kissed, and covered with a Band-Aid. This time I got something completely different. Teddy picked me up as if he were going to carry me back to the house. While my legs were wrapped around him, he pushed his body against mine where my back was pinned to the side of the abandoned house. He started to kiss me like I had seen adults do and started dry humping me. I was so scared and completely became numb. I knew what he was doing was a bad thing and I didn't know how to process that. He just kept groping me and touching me and kissing me until he finally stopped and put me down. With a sneer, he said, "Tag...you're it!" He took off running and yelling, "I found Morgan! She's it!" until he got back to Uncle Sambo's yard. I didn't move. I sat down and cried. Hide and go seek was never played like this when I was with my real family. How could my mother do this to me and Logan? Why did she keep us from our family? In about five minutes, Syleena and Brandon, Teddy's older brother, came and found me still in the same spot.

"Morgan, what's wrong?" Syleena asked. I said nothing as I still cried.

"Oh look, her knee's bleeding," Brandon said. "C'mon let's take her back to her mom." Brandon reached for me and I

lunged at him screaming until he backed up. Syleena
grabbed my hands and said, "Okay, okay, I got you."
"What did I do?" Brandon asked.
"You're a boy," Syleena answered.
When Brandon, Syleena, and I got back to Uncle Sambo's
yard, all of the kids were sitting around waiting on us. Logan
was sitting with Liyah, another of Uncle Sambo's nieces who
was the same age as we were. She ran over to me and
hugged me.
"Hold on, Logan," Syleena said. "We gotta take her to your
mom because she fell."
Logan backed up and walked into the house with me.
Syleena explained to my mom what happened. She was
directed by Aunt Toni, Uncle Sambo's wife, to where the first
aid kit was. Mom took me into the bathroom, used alcohol
to clean my knee, and covered it with a Band-Aid.
"Mommy, I wanna go home!" I exclaimed.
"Why?" she asked. "You're not having fun with the other
kids?"
"No! I want Grandmama!"
"We'll leave in a few hours," she stated. When she said that
I bawled hard.
"What is wrong with you?" Mom asked. I was about to tell
her what Teddy did until I saw him standing in the doorway
of the bathroom making gestures that he would beat me up
if I told. My mom looked behind her and saw him standing
there.
"Is she alright, Miss Belle?" Teddy asked trying to act
concerned. He stood there in his orange t-shirt and jeans
dripping in sweat.
Smiling, my mom said, "She's fine, Teddy. See, Mo, Teddy's
worried about you. Why do you want to leave?"
I looked at him and he just glared at me devilishly. I looked
away and instantly stopped crying. I was devastated. My

mom towered over me in her red jumpsuit. Standing at five feet ten inches and weighing 210 pounds, my mom's brown sugar skin, wide nose and Jheri curl often left a lot of people questioning if I was her birth daughter or not because we looked nothing alike. As she was putting all of the First Aid supplies away, she said to me, "You and your sister will be leaving soon. Don't worry. But I want you to have some fun before we leave, okay?"

I nodded my head. Teddy finally walked away. For the rest of the day there, I stayed in the den.

We finally went home around nine o'clock that night. Logan and I were laying in the back seat (before it was a law to wear a seat belt or be in booster seats). Mom was holding Joseph in the front seat while Daniel drove us back to Grandmama's house. With a cigarette behind his right ear, he looked toward the back to see if Logan and I were asleep. Then he looked at our mother. With a low grumble, I guess trying to keep his voice low for us not to hear, he asked Mom, "You coming back with me after you take them to your mother's?"

"Sure," she said.

"See if she'll keep Joseph too," he requested.

"I can't," she answered. "She told me she's not watching no more of my kids."

"Really?" he asked.

"Yeah. I tell you...the biggest mistake of my life was having those two with their father. I should've aborted them like I did the others after them."

"Belle...don't you think that's a bit harsh?"

"No. Every time I look at them, it's a constant reminder of *him* and *his* family. They're his color, have his eyes...just everyday..."

"Well, I think they're beautiful. Besides, they fit right along well in my family. From this day forth, they're my girls. DNA don't matter."

"I wish I would've met you sooner. That way all of my kids would have the same biological father. But it is what it is I guess."

We pulled up at the intersection of California Avenue and Brighton Road about to make a right onto North Charles Street when Daniel abruptly put on the brakes. Mom started screaming and I sat straight up. I looked out of the window to see my father and his brother, my uncle, in another car blocking Daniel from driving forward. My father and uncle jumped out of a blue Chevy Nova and walked over to Daniel.

"Nigga, park *my* car and get the fuck out of it!" my dad yelled.

Logan and I sat up in the backseat and watched the whole scene.

"Don't do this, Ray!" Mom yelled.

"What da fuck is he doin' drivin' my car, Belle?!" Dad yelled. "I told you to put the car in your name until I got my shit straight with DMV, but you ridin' around lettin' *this* nigga drive my shit?!"

"If it's in my name it's *my* car!" Mom yelled.

"Bitch...! Get the fuck out my car! Both of y'all!"

"Hold up, Ray," my uncle said. "Your girls are back here."

Dad looked in the back and saw Logan and me.

"Earl, take my girls and put them in my car!" my father yelled. "Why the fuck they ain't home anyway, Belle?!"

Daniel got out of the car, "Yo, man, you want your ride?" He said taunting my dad with the car keys. I didn't see anything else because Uncle Earl grabbed me and Logan out of the backseat of the light blue Grand Prix we were riding in and quickly put us in our father's car. Logan and I looked out of the window and saw our father and Daniel fighting. Mom just stood there holding our brother Joseph and yelling.

Uncle Earl broke up the fight and a bunch of traffic started to pile up. Dad said something to Uncle Earl and he backed off. Somehow, my dad got the keys to the Grand Prix and drove off. Uncle Earl jumped back into the car we were in, told us to get in the back, and took us to Grandmama's house. They left Mom, Joseph, and Daniel on the corner.

We got to Grandmama's house on Strauss Street and she looked confused to see Uncle Earl bring us home. In her green housecoat, she asked, "Where's their mother?" Uncle Earl replied, "I don't know, Ma'am. Ray told me to bring them here." Uncle Earl opened the car door to let us out. He always looked like he had a scowl on his face behind his beard and Mr. T-like body. We walked passed him and ran into Grandmama's house; the place we called home. I ran upstairs to see where Grandpa was and found him in the bathroom shaving for the night.
"Hey, Roo!" he said with a toothless smile. Grandpa was a slim man with a bald head who was never seen without a hat, a drink, or his pistol.
"Hi, Grandpa," I said.
"Ya gotta go to the bathroom?" he asked with a half of face full of shaving cream.
"No," I answered.
"Hmm, ya watchin' ya ol' granddad shave, eh?"
I nodded my head yes.
"Well, ya need ta be getting' ta bed. Where's ya Ma?"
I shrugged my shoulders.
"Ya don't know?" he asked. I nodded no. Grandpa put the razor down on the bathroom sink and went to the top of the stairs and yelled, "Gabby! Where dat gal at?!"
"I don't know!" Grandmama yelled back up the stairs.
"These youngins need ta go ta bed! It's late!"
"I know that, Willie James! Hush!" Grandmama yelled back.

Grandpa started mumbling back in the bathroom to finish shaving. I walked up to the third floor to where Logan and I shared a room. As dirty as I was, I jumped in my bed anyway. Logan was right behind me and jumped in hers. She went right to sleep as soon as her head hit the pillow.

I was almost asleep until I heard a bunch of commotion downstairs. I jumped out of bed to see what was going on. Logan was still asleep and I was about to wake her up, but something kept me from doing that. I ran all the way downstairs to the kitchen and found Mom and Grandpa fist-fighting. I instantly started crying as my mother was exchanging blows with my grandfather. My grandmother was yelling for them to stop and my Aunt Grace, who also lived with us, was pulling on my mother. When they parted, Grandpa pulled his gun out and said, "Get out my damn house!"

"Willie, no!" Grandmama yelled.

"C'mon, Willie," Aunt Grace begged. None of his children ever called him Dad. "Don't do this! Please!"

Grandmama realized I was there and picked me up. "Willie! Not in front of the baby!"

"Git out, Belle!" he yelled waving his gun at her. "You's nuthin' but trouble!"

"Fine!" Mom yelled back. "Let me get me and my kids' clothes and we'll be out your house!"

"You ain't taking those kids, Belle! They stay here!"

Mom went to her room with Aunt Grace behind her. Grandpa was still yelling and carrying his gun. Grandmama held onto me closely as I cried.

"Stop crying, Gal," she whispered. "You ain't going nowhere."

*********************************************

"Mo...Mo..." Lance said shaking me awake. "Baby, you're

crying in your sleep. Wake up."

"Hmm? What time is it?" I asked.

"It's 9pm," Lance answered. "What were you dreaming about?"

"Oh...nothing," I answered.

"Nothing my ass. Mo, you were crying."

"Just don't worry about it. I'm okay. Are the babies up?"

"Of course. They've been fed and cleaned for over two hours now."

"Okay. I'm getting up."

"For what? Morgan, what the hell was all of that about? What were you dreaming about?!"

I sat up in my bed and said, "The dreams...they're nightmares...about my past...my childhood."

"Mo, you really need to see someone about this," Lance said. "It's not healthy for you. You've been holding on to pain you need to let go of."

"How do you *erase* pain?! Huh?! How do you erase what you've had inflicted on you as an innocent child?! *How?!* What is psycho-babble gonna do for me except make me relive a part of my life that I wanna forget about?!" I jumped out of bed and went to the bathroom and locked the door. Lance tried to open the door and realized it was locked. On the other side of the door, he said, "Mo...we can fix this...together. Please don't shut me out."

"Give me a minute, Lance," I stated. "Leave me alone." It became silent on the other side of the door. I assumed that Lance went on and respected my request. Then, a voice popped up that spooked me.

"Why aren't you being truthful?" It was that black-eyed reflection of mine in the mirror. I didn't look up.

"Go...away! Get out of my head! You're nothing but a figment of my imagination," I yelled.

"Ha, ha, ha, ha! You believe I am, don't you?" it asked. "I

am *you*. Your conscience, your heart, and your soul. Why don't you face me? Face yourself! The...true...Morgan!" I looked into the mirror and was stuck. I looked at that awful being. "My eyes are black because it represents your heart; dark...cold...soulless. You'll never...*never*...get rid of me as long as you hold contempt in your heart." I closed my eyes for twenty seconds. When I reopened them, that reflection was gone. I left the bathroom and went out to the living room. Alanna was watching videos, Chantel was on the phone, and Lance was in his favorite chair holding the twins. His eyes met mine and without saying anything, we told each other we love each other.

## Chapter Four

"Mrs. Brooks, I want to thank you so much for helping me get me on track," my client Diamond said as she sat across from me at *Shining Star* in my office. Diamond is Quiana's daughter; my ex-boyfriend's current girlfriend. Though she had another representative, and despite Quiana's reservations that I would be able to help her, Diamond came a long way in a year. She found and kept a steady job and continued cosmetology school and was able to find her own apartment.

"You know you owe that to your rep," I answered.

"True," she agreed. "But you kept pressing me when she couldn't. That's why I'm thanking you."

"No problem," I laughed. "So...what're you really here for?" Sitting back in the black leather chair across from my desk, Diamond said, "My mom is thinking of leaving Kevin...and I don't want her to."

Puzzled, I asked, "Why? I mean...why is it bothering you?"

"Mrs. Brooks, Kevin has been so positive and influential to me. He's been like a father to me. I don't want them to break up."

"Diamond, as much as we like to hold on to what's dear to us, sometimes we don't get what we want. But the Kevin that I know wouldn't walk away from you. If you've built a relationship with him, he'll stay true to you."

"Really? You think so?" Diamond questioned.

"I know so," I reassured. "Before we stopped being friends, Kevin was always the one who was there. He stays true to who's true with him."

Nodding in agreement, Diamond said, "Okay." Standing up in her red and white tank top and blue jean capris that accentuated her 21 year-old full-figured body, she said, "I'll take your word on it."

"Umm, Diamond," I began, "next time you come here to do business, don't wear that tank top. You have too much on display."

Laughing, Diamond said, "Mrs. Brooks, I have my jacket."

"Well then put it on!" I said smiling.

"Yes, ma'am," she said walking out of the office door. My desk phone alerted me that Mrs. Lopez was calling me from her office extension so I answered.

"Hi, Mrs. Lopez," I greeted."

"Hello there, Morgan," she replied in her rich, Spanish accent. "I have someone here in my office looking for you. Do you still have your client?"

"Umm, no," I answered. "No one is here now. But I don't have anyone on my schedule who I'm supposed to meet until 1:30."

"Hmm, I see," Mrs. Lopez answered. "Well, I think you can make time for Miss Reyes, right?"

It couldn't be! "Autumn Reyes?!"

"That's who she said she is," Mrs. Lopez answered.

"Oh, yes! Send her down! Thank you!" I couldn't believe she was actually here to see me. So many years had passed and there was so much we had to catch up on. I stood up and walked around my desk to walk to the office door to wait for her. When I opened the door, she was already standing on the other side. There stood my short, thick friend from college. Wearing a white tunic and an orange ankle length skirt with white open toe sandals and her hair in beach curls, Autumn stood with this big smile on her face.

"I can't believe my eyes!" she exclaimed. "Morgan Chambers!"

"You mean Morgan Brooks," I corrected. We embraced each other for about twenty seconds and then I invited her in my office. She sat down on the navy blue leather couch against the wall close to the door and I sat next to her.

"So what do I owe the pleasure of this visit?" I asked.

"Oh, I didn't know I needed a reason to see my old friend," Autumn replied. "It's been seven...years. Seven, Mo! I mean, c'mon. You're married with children, making a name for yourself with this business, and doing something worthwhile."

"And you're not doing bad yourself," I added. "Worked for Vibe, New York Times, and started your own business."

"And divorced, may I add," Autumn interjected.

"When did you get married?" I asked in shock.

"Three years ago," Autumn answered. "I married a fellow journalist at Vibe. We just finalized our divorce three months ago."

"Oh, I'm sorry," I said.

"No, don't be," she replied. "Mark was a lot of things wonderful...except straight."

"What?!"

Nodding, Autumn said, "Yep. Mark came clean to me after our second anniversary."

I was totally baffled. "So, what happened? Did you catch him or something?"

"No. We were having dinner and I brought up having kids one day. In the middle of my nostalgia, Mark stopped me and said *'Autie, I can't do this to you anymore. You're too beautiful and deserving of someone who's gonna give you what you deserve in life. And having a gay husband isn't what you deserve.'* At that point, I felt like my heart and lungs collapsed. I thought my ears were deceiving my brain."

"Oh, Autumn...I'm so, so, sorry!"

"Don't be. Mark taught me a lot of good things about our line of work and we're still friends."

"But if he knew he was gay, why did he marry you?"

"He said he knew being gay was a sin and he wanted to be

right. So he saw a lot of me in him and felt that if he could marry a mirror image of himself, then he could 'cure' his homosexuality and grow to love women and learn how to be straight. He also didn't want to disappoint his family."

"Forgive me for asking, but, what was it like sleeping with him?"

"Haaa, ha, ha, ha! Girl, I was his first!"

"Wait, I'm confused. What do you mean?"

"I mean...I was his first heterosexual experience!"

"So technically...he was a virgin?"

"Yup! And I get to take that with me forever!"

"So what was that like for you? For him?"

"Girl, it was something. Being the first for a man is sensational! He's a wonderful lover and wasn't afraid to try anything. He said the feeling of being with a woman is one that he'll cherish and never forget. But he's attracted to men and that's something that a traditional marriage won't fix."

"But didn't you feel like you were being an experiment?"

"You know...after he came clean to me and told me, I did. But Mark told me he loved me and was in love with me and loved everything I brought to him about loving women."

"But he'd still prefer to have another sausage in his butt or mouth?"

"Stop, Mo! In all honesty, I thought I turned him gay. But he revealed to me some things I overlooked because I was so caught up in him and I recognized he's been gay the whole time before and after we were married."

"And you're not upset?"

"No. I'm not. Disappointed? Yes. Because he left me for someone else. In the end, regardless of how he chooses to live, he left me for someone else. Now at the age of 33, I have to start all over again before my eggs dry up."

If it were me, I would've been pissed. I commend Autumn for her strength to accept her ex-husband was gay. I put my

hand on hers and squeezed it to let her know I'm here for
her in any way she needed.

"So..." I began, "how long are you in town?"

"For two weeks," Autumn replied. "I have to meet with
some execs at *EShaMon* who are going to help me market
my business. It's not very easy to sell a new journalism
company."

I paused for a second. "You're going to *EShaMon*?" I
questioned.

"Yeah...why?" Autumn questioned. I wondered if she knew
Kevin Littleton was one of the execs.

"Um...do you know Kevin Littleton?" I asked.

"Sort of. I've heard he's done magnificent work and he's one
of the masterminds of the company."

"Well, that is true. Kevin is brilliant."

Shifting in her seat, Autumn said, "Oh? You've worked with
him before? Heard of his work?"

Clearing my throat, I replied, "Kevin and I used to be
childhood friends. We grew up together. Even dated before I
got married."

"For real?"

"Yes. But I wouldn't go over there telling him about that or
that you know me. It didn't end well between us."

"Oh, I see. Don't worry I won't say anything. So...when am I
going to see your family? And Logan? How's she?"

"If you have time this evening you can stop by my house
and I'll introduce you to everyone. Logan and her family are
doing well. Her family is beautiful."

"Do you think she'll be able to come over?"

"She should be able to."

"That sounds great! I want to hang loose for a while before
I head back home."

"Where are you living now?"

"I live in Austin, Texas. Just me and my younger brother."

Autumn's brother, Neil, is an eccentric and talented musician. He's making a name for himself in the music industry with his ability to sing, play multiple instruments, and songwriting. He was featured a couple of times on major music networks and has appeared as a guest artist with many big names.

"How did you convince him to leave Philly?"

"Oh it didn't take much; trust me! Ha, ha, ha! He got sick of the weather and wanted to make a change in his life."

"But isn't Philly one of the music satellites in the country?"

"Not like it used to be. I mean, there are still people who can get on in Philly, but if you're not in L.A., Atlanta, New York, Chicago, or Miami, you're not really gonna get *on*. Besides...I like having him with me."

"Well, good for both of you." My intercom buzzed. Lana, the dedicated receptionist, informed me that my next appointment had arrived.

"Well, that's my cue to leave," Autumn announced. We both stood at the same time.

"Wait, I have to give you my cell phone number," I said. I jot down my cell phone number on a post-it note and gave it to her. "Call me at 5. I'll be home by then."

"I will. Can't wait 'til later!" We hugged each other and I walked her to the front door. On my way back to my office, I walked with my next client and proceeded with remainder of my work day.

\*\*\*\*\*\*\*\*\*\*\*\*\*\*\*\*\*\*\*\*\*\*\*\*\*\*\*\*\*\*\*\*\*\*\*\*\*\*\*\*\*\*\*\*\*\*\*\*\*\*\*\*

I arrived home early at 4:00pm. With my work schedule being 7:30am-4pm, this gives me enough time to get pick up the twins from day care two blocks from our home and to spend time with the kids while their father is on his crazy shift for the next few months. Since Autumn was in town, I was able to leave at 3:00pm today since my schedule was cleared and I had some PTO time I was able use today. I pulled into the driveway and parked my Durango. I got out of my car carefully because my feet were killing me and I forgot to bring my sneakers I usually wore before and after work so I wouldn't have sore feet from wearing dress shoes all day. I opened the driver's side passenger door to lift my happy little girl out of her car seat. Jayda was all smiles with her thick, curly hair I managed to put in four ponytail afro puffs early in the morning. Her little vanilla, round body wiggled excitedly as I picked her up and gave her kisses on her little chubby cheeks. I got her on my hip, closed and locked the door, then walked around the back of the truck to get Jayden. He, too, was awake and excited to see me. While balancing his sister in my left arm, I lifted Jayden out of his detachable car seat and sat him on the pavement so I could close the rear passenger door. I used my key remote to lock the truck, picked up Jayden, and walked toward the side door to get into the house. I had to sit Jayden down again to unlock the house door and I started laughing at myself. Juggling to get the kids in was always a job in itself.

After I unlocked the door and pushed it open, I carried the babies in and closed the door with my hip. Jayda was reaching for hair at this point and trying to grab one of my dreds. I sat Jayden down again once we got into the living room so I could put Jayda in the pack and play. I sat down on the couch and started to unbuckle Jayden. Once I got him out, I gave him his kisses and sat him down in the pack and play with his sister. I was on my way to the powder room when a sound from Alanna's room diverted me. I walked toward her bedroom door and paused. I stood there with my ears open. I know that girl ain't.....! I tried to turn the knob but it was locked. Little did any of the kids know Lance and I had a key to unlock all of the doors inside the house in the event of an emergency. I quickly walked into my room and got the key out of my jewelry box and scurried back across down the hall. I unlocked Alanna's bedroom door and opened it to find her spread eagle on her back in her bed with her boyfriend filling the void. With the music playing, they didn't know I was there.

"I know you better get your ass outta her and get the hell outta my house!" I yelled.

Startled and embarrassed, Alanna's boyfriend, Shakim, jumped off of Alanna and scrambled out of the bed stark naked grabbing the sheet that was crumpled up at the foot of the bed to cover himself. Alanna took her pillow and wrapped her body around it to cover her ballerina body.

"Mo-Ma!" she exclaimed. "I—I—,"

"—Shakim, get your things and get out my house before I put a hot bullet in your ass!" I threatened.

"Uh..yes, ma'am! I'm sorry—"he sputtered. His 5'7" dark brown frame scrambled to get his clothes.

"—Sorry my ass! Hurry up before I call her father!"

Grabbing his boxers off the floor, he hurriedly put them on. I wasn't moving. Little did they know, I was trying to save them from Lance though, I threatened to call him. I could've given him time to dress without my presence, but if Lance would've come in, all hell would've broken loose.

"Boy, just put your pants and shoes on and be out," I ordered. Shakim jumped in his pants and shoes and ran out of the house holding his pants up and with his t-shirt in his mouth. Alanna was frozen on the bed wrapped around her pillow. I walked over to her windows and opened them. All the while, Alanna kept her eyes on me.

"Girl," I began, "get a shower, change your sheets, and meet me in the living room before your father gets home." I walked out of her room and closed the door behind me. I didn't go off on her like a typical mother...or step-mother. Why? At 16, I was in Kevin's mother's house doing the same thing and at 18, I was in college wildin' out. So I understood completely how the opportunity presented itself and she took it.

The next thirty minutes passed and Alanna finally joined me and her twin siblings in the living room. She sat in her father's recliner across from me as I curled up with Jayden in the corner of the over-sized living room furniture that's been there since Lance and I started dating. Alanna put on a long, strapless black and white striped dress that draped down to her ankles. She didn't make eye contact with me and started fiddling with her manicured French tip fingernails. As I was feeding the round little baby boy, I looked at Alanna.

"Lanni, I don't want you worrying about me telling your father because I'm not," I began. "I understand totally why you took advantage. You know our work schedules and you had the opportunity. I did the same thing and so did your father and many more people besides us. And every parent tells their children...and step-children...not to have sex in their house. However, the children...and step-children...will eventually break that rule. You are 16 and Shakim is 17 and full of hormones. However, I can't let you disrespect our home like this, Alanna."

"Mo-Ma," Alanna started with a quivering voice, "I'm so, so, sorry. I truly apologize. I promise I'll never do that again under your roof."

"I accept your apology. Like I said, I'm not going to tell your father. Now...can you take Jayda out of the pack and play and change her please? I have to get ready for a friend of mine to stop by."

Without saying a word, Alanna done as I asked her to with

her baby sister. I had to get that visual out of my head of my step-daughter getting rammed by her boyfriend aggressively. But I was going to do whatever I could to purge that image. My cell phone started ringing. I extended my right arm to middle of the couch where it lay and picked it up. It was Logan.

"Hey, Cookie," I answered.

"What's going on, Mo?" she replied.

"I'm feeding Jayden right now. I tried calling you when I got out of the office earlier."

"Yeah, I know. I was having a parent teacher conference with one of A.J.'s teachers."

"How'd it go?"

Taking a deep breath, Logan commenced to tell me how A.J. has been acting out in school. Arriving to classes late after the bell, turning in half done homework, not participating in class, and back talking the teachers. "I just don't know what to do at this point. It's so early in the school year. If I don't do something now, it'll only get worse. I can't have him in 7$^{th}$ grade acting like a damn fool before he even gets started."

"Have you talked to Brian about this?"

"Not yet. He's at a conference with the Georgia Department of Education. But I'm worried because...I think he's upset that he didn't have a chance to know his father."

"Did he say that?"

"He's been asking me a bunch of questions lately."

"So you haven't told him what happened when he was a baby?"

"Yes," Whispering, Logan proceeded with, "But not the whole truth. What do I look like telling him *I* killed his father? Even if it was out of self-defense?"

I couldn't fathom the idea. "Geez, Cookie, I don't know what to tell you on that. But at some point, you have to tell him before his nutball grandmother does."

"Which one?"

We both started laughing. Lance's mother and my mother were two women who hid behind religion to justify their behaviors. "Before I forget, Autumn came by my office. She's going to come here sometime between 5pm. She wants to see you."

"Oh, she's here?! Finally! I'll be there for sure!"

"Well it's already 4 o'clock. Ya might wanna light a fire under your butt and get here. It's not like you have a small family."

"Ha ha…very funny."

"Make sure you bring Brian."

"Uh, I don't know. He's still pretty bummed about our spat."

"Logan, that was a week ago! We've made up before I even left that day!"

"Yeah, and we've talked plenty of times after that too. He still hasn't gotten over it."

"Well, what do I need to do to fix this? I have mad love for Brian."

"Let me handle my husband. Don't worry, we'll be there."

Jayden started fidgeting in my lap. When I looked down, half of his formula was gone and he wanted to be burped. "Logan, let me finish feeding Jayden. Just be here when you can."

"No problem. See ya."

I took the bottle out of Jayden's mouth and set it on the table. At three months old, he already weighed in at 11 pounds and was so round and fat, he looked like a baby Sumo wrestler. I put him up on my shoulder to pat his back and help him burp. Just like his sister, he was obsessed with my hair. I loved feeling his soft, baby skin and the baby smell that exuded from his hair and skin. More and more he was looking like his father and I loved every moment of holding my son. Jayden finally burped and I gave the mommy congratulatory. Just as I was pulling him off of my shoulder, he had another burp followed with milk pouring out of his mouth and onto my chest. Aahh...the joys of motherhood.

Chantel came in like a ball of energy. She blew through the side door like Flash Gordon with her yellow outfit that I didn't recognize from her wardrobe.

"Hey, Mo-Ma!" Chantel yelled as she ran to her room. There's no telling what she was up to, but normally when she done that, she was trying to avoid her father and go somewhere he didn't approve.

"Chantel! Come back in here!" I yelled. Within ten seconds, she appeared and stood in front of me.

"Where's the fire?" I asked sarcastically still trying to wipe baby puke off of my shirt.

"Nowhere," Chantel answered.

"What's the hurry?" I questioned.

"I'm going with Octavia and her sister to the mall."

"And who else?"

"Mo-Ma...it's just them."

"And...who...else?"

Exhaling sharply, Chantel replied, "And Jamelle, DeMarcus, and Tramarvious."

"Are one of these boys who you've been talking to me about?"

"Yes."

"Please tell me he's one with a somewhat normal name."

Laughing, Chantel replied, "I'm sorry but Tramarvious is the guy I was talking to you about."

"And you all are going to the mall? Which one?"

"North Point Mall."

"Did you talk to your father about this?"

"Mo-Ma, he's going to say no!"

"Why?"

"Because he don't want me involved with Tramarvious."

"So you want me to get yelled at for saying okay go to the mall with your friends and to hook up with some boys, one of them whom doesn't sit well with your father, before you ran it by him?"

"Mo-Ma, pleeeaaassseeee!!! I'll be home before he gets home. I promise."

"Do you know what time he's getting home?"

"Umm...no..."

"So how can you tell me you'll get home before he gets home and you don't know what time he's coming home?"

"What time is Daddy coming home?"

"Probably around 6:30. And you know as well as I do you're not going to make it back here before he comes home. Tell you what...go to the mall and be back by 9. Just call him and tell him where you're going so he won't blame me for keeping secrets."

Smiling broadly, Chantel answered, "I will! Thank you!"

"Please don't make me regret it."

Chantel came toward me, leaned in to gave me a hug, and kissed Jayden on the forehead. Next thing she was out the door. Alanna came into the living room with Jayda. She dressed Jayda in a lime green and white polka dot dress and left her feet without booties. Alanna sat on the other end of the couch with Jayda on her lap.

"Mo-Ma, I've been thinking it may be time for me to move out," Alanna stated.

"Really? Why?" I asked.

"Because I'm grown—"

"—Stop right there! *You* are *not* grown!"

"I'm just saying," Alanna began, "Shakim is gonna be 18 years old and I'm not trying to do anything that's gonna cause our relationship to fall. And the relationship with Dad too."

"What makes you think you're ready to move out? Because you got caught screwing in your father's house?"

"Nobody else I know have this problem."

"Really?"

"Yes...really."

"If that was the case why weren't you at Shakim's house?"

"Because I'm tired of going over there."

"And when you're there screwing him, where's his parents?"

"His dad don't care, but we can't do that while his father's home."

"Of course his dad don't care! Fathers typically support their son screwing a female! What about his mother?"

"He don't live with his mother."

"Oh, I see. So you wanted a change in scenery, huh? Before you say anything else, let me share something with you: just because you wanna get some whenever you want to doesn't constitute you as grown. And a piece of meat shouldn't get you all up in a tizzy because you can't get it under your father's roof. Now your little friends might be able to get screwed in their parents' homes, but not here. I'm trying to save you from yourself and your father. You wanna screw with Shakim, get a damn hotel room or keep going to his house."

"Man, I—"

"—Say something else, Alanna, and I will be telling your father!"

Alanna sat still and held her little sister. I could tell she wanted to say something else because she kept biting her bottom lip.

The doorbell rang and Alanna jumped up to go to the front door. A few seconds later, Autumn was walking behind Alanna with a very handsome man. I stood up with

Jayden in my arm and leaned down to hug my friend.

"Please excuse the baby puke," I said.

"Girl, no problem," Autumn answered. "I want you to meet my business partner Mark Lattimore."

I paused. Was this the Mark she was talking about? I guess the expression on my face asked because Autumn nodded yes. From a physical attraction, I could tell why she was attracted to him. He and I stood eye-to-eye, he had a very neatly trimmed beard, a clean shaven head, had smooth chocolate skin, and bright, white, straight teeth. He put me in the mind of Taye Diggs and when he said hello, his voice was very smooth. He extended his hand out to shake mine and though he had a strong grip, his hands were very soft. Not a sign of a callous on his palm.

"This is one of my step-daughters, Alanna," I introduced. "Alanna, this is my friend from college, Autumn, and her colleague, Mark."

"Hi, it's nice to meet y'all," Alanna replied.

"This little guy is Jayden and that little lady Alanna is holding is Jayda," I said introducing them to my twin babies.

"They...are...too...adorable!" Autumn squealed. "Let me hold one of them, please!"

"Well, take my little man," I suggested. "I'm going to go change my shirt. It's starting to smell like sour milk. You both can have a seat. I'll be right back."

I handed Jayden to Autumn and she was tickled pink. I walked into my bedroom to change my shirt. I decided to get one of Lance's t-shirts from his drawer. At that moment, I recognized I never changed out of my work clothes at all. So, I hurriedly changed into a pair of black sweatpants and put on a black t-shirt. When I walked back into the living room, Mark was holding Jayda and Autumn was awestruck with Jayden. I noticed Alanna wasn't in the room.

"Hey, Mo, Alanna said she'd be back," Autumn reported.

"Thanks for letting me know," I said. "She didn't tell me she had somewhere to go nor is she scheduled to work today." As I sat down in my husband's recliner, Mark said, "You have a lovely home."

"Thank you very much," I replied. "My husband had this set up all by himself."

"Oh he did?" Mark inquired.

"Yes...he did. When we got married, I just moved in with my belongings. Everything else I owned before we got together has been put in the den or scattered in the other rooms. Whatever didn't belong, I gave to my sister."

"Wow. That's awesome," Mark said. "So, you're the infamous Morgan Chambers my Autie has talked so much about? I feel like I already know you."

"Oh is that right? I hope it was nothing bad," I said.

"Well, she told me how you were there for her when no one else was. And...that horrible ordeal you all had in college."

"I hope you understand, Mo, Mark's my best friend. I share a lot with him," Autumn added.

"I can understand, girl. I'm not upset about that," I replied.

"So where is everyone?" Autumn asked.

"Logan said she'll be here when she can. Lance will be here by 6:30," I stated.

"So what's it like being a mother? I'm still shocked that you're a mom!" Autumn bellowed.

Taking a deep breath, I said, "It's an experience and a blessing. Not to mention I came into this relationship with a man who already had four kids."

"Oh wow!" Mark said. "Are they all by the same woman?"

"Mark!" Autumn said slapping his knee.

I laughed. "It's okay, Autumn. Yes, Mark, they're all by the same woman."

"That's a rarity," he said.

"And I love it! Though their mother isn't the sharpest tool in the shed, I don't have to be overwhelmed with two or more baby mamas," I said. "So, Mark, do you mind me asking you a question or two?"

"It depends on what the questions are and if I agree to answer," he replied.

"Why aren't you and my girl still together?"

Autumn looked at me as if to tell me to shut up.

Clearing his throat, Mark said, "I, uh, am a gay man. But I'm pretty sure you already knew that."

"What makes you certain I knew?"

"C'mon...I know Autumn told you when she met you this morning."

"No...she didn't." At this time, Autumn was looking at me like I was a bat out of hell.

"Well, Miss Morgan, I love the hell out of your girl here. We were married for two years before I came clean about who I was to her. I didn't want to keep going on in my life living on both sides of the fence hurting this beautiful woman."

"Mark, I don't get it. You're a handsome, and seemingly intelligent man. Why did you do that to her?"

"You don't get it. I love, and I mean I *love* Autumn. But I can't be married to a woman and have sexual desires to be with another man."

I shook my head. "So you don't want kids?"

"Yes one day. I tried to convince Autumn to be my donor but her family values and standards won't allow us to."

"That's right," Autumn chimed in. "I'd do anything I can for him, except have children for him."

My side door opened and closed. Next thing, four children and three adults popped up in my living room. Logan, Brian, their children, and my husband all came barreling through. I stood up to walk to my husband and kiss him. Logan and Autumn were greeting each other and doing introductions. I introduced Autumn and Mark to my husband. Lance then pulled me to the side and asked to speak with me in our bedroom. We walked down the hallway and entered our room. Lance closed the door behind him and walked toward our lounge to sit on and I followed him.

"Baby, what's been going on here today?" Lance asked.

"The same stuff," I answered. "Why?"

"Well, Chantel called me and said she'd be at the mall for a couple of hours with her friends and asked me if I wanted anything. Then I just get a text message from Alanna saying she was going to be staying with your cousin Kenya for the weekend."

*That little female!* I thought. "Honey, Chantel is just being herself. The social butterfly. Alanna on the other hand is on some crap right now I don't wanna delve into."

"Like what?"

"She wants to move out."

"What?! Why?!"

"She thinks she's *grown* and feels she needs her own space."

"Well, something brought that on. Did you ask?"

"No," I said lying to my husband.

"You know I'm not buying that."

"Lance, they're being typical teenage girls."

"Yeah, but according to your family you weren't the typical teenage girl."

"My sister was," I said laughing. "Seriously, they're just trying to have some fun for the weekend. That's all."

"Hmm. Okay. So that lady out there...Autumn...she's the one from college?"

"Yup."

"And that guy is..."

"Her gay ex-husband."

"Huh?"

"Let's go out and learn more."

"Okay. Oh wait one more thing. Brian and I talked about that whole ordeal with what happened at his house two weeks ago."

"And...?"

"And...he said he understand siblings fight. He fought his, I fought mine. But he's not about to have you, me, or anyone disrespect his wife, their kids, and their home. I told him I'm not about anyone disrespecting my wife and kids period. So next time he has an issue with you, he needs to take it up with me...like a man." Kissing me on my forehead, Lance said, "Now, let's go socialize so I can get them out of our house and I can get into you."

Kissing him back, I said, "As much as I know you'd like it, that ain't happening tonight. I have a visitor who'll be around for the next 4 to 7 days."

"Naw, naw, naw!" Lance said disappointedly. "That can't be! You're off schedule at least five days!"

"Well, she decided to come early, darling."

Lance and I walked back into the living room.

For the next two hours, Lance, Brian, Mark, Logan, Autumn, and I laughed and talked. That evening had been one of the best evenings we've had amongst other adults besides my cousin Ramona and her brothers and Brian and his siblings. The guys eventually went into the den to talk and Autumn, Logan, and I stayed in the living room. The babies were starting to get restless so Logan offered to hold Jayden to rock him to sleep and I held Jayda and rocked her to sleep. Logan's kids were off in the twins' room playing games and so far, they were doing well with the exception of A.J. coming out saying he was tired of babysitting on numerous occasions. Flipping her hair back over her shoulder, Autumn said, "I can't believe how well you two are doing! I'm so proud of y'all...and a little jealous."

"Jealous?" Logan asked. "Why?"

"Because this is what I've always wanted," Autumn said. "To be married with children and have the career of my dream."

"Well, what's the deal with Mark? Why don't you try to tame that hunk of chocolate?" Logan inquired. I held in my laugh by biting my lower lip. Clearing her throat, Autumn said, "Umm, Mark is my ex-husband. We've been divorced for a little over a year now."

"What da hell?" Logan asked.

"Umm, Logan, Mark is...gay," Autumn confessed.

Logan said nothing. Her mouth dropped and she had a blank stare for about fifteen seconds. She finally voiced, "Gay? Mark's gay? How could you not know that before? Why did you marry a gay man?"

"Well, quite simple. I didn't know he was gay. Had I'd known, I'd never went that route with him. But there's so much to him and I never would've guessed that or even speculated that. Nobody would've really known that."

"Pardon me for asking, but how was the sex life?" Logan questioned.

"Umm, Cookie," I interjected.

"No, no, Morgan, it's fine," Autumn reassured. "Logan, Mark was a heterosexual virgin. I broke him in, I was his first—"

"No, you were an experiment," Logan interrupted.

"Logan!" I stated.

"No, no!" Logan said sternly. "Autumn...c'mon! We go back 15 years now. Before I left and moved to Charlotte with Amari, you allowed yourself to be in some fucked up relationships. You dated a notorious cheater, allowed a dude to beat on you, had a total bum who mooched off of you, a criminal, and now you're here telling us you married a gay man?"

I was floored. Logan never criticized anyone for their relationships or lifestyles until now.

"What has gotten into you?" I asked her.

Teary eyed, Autumn said, "It's cool, Morgan. I get this from my family all of the time. Let me explain something to you, Logan, what I do with my life is *my* life! Yes, I made mistakes, have fallen for the misfits of society, and completely wear my heart on my sleeve because I'm *desperate* for love. I want to be loved and to give love and to be happy. Maybe I am a magnet for troubled men or maybe I'm not afraid to put myself out there until love finds me."

"But haven't you learned not to jump in feet first?" Logan inquired. "Autumn, you're too pretty, intelligent, and have a lot going on with you that the right man would cherish forever."

Standing up, Autumn said, "Look at me, Logan. Look at me! I'm five foot three, 150 pounds, and I'm not the best looking female in the world. I'm not the ideal woman for many men. The guys I'm interested in show no interest in me whatsoever. I'm not going to keep putting myself out there in hopes I get the man of my dreams. So if the misfit approaches me, so be it."

Putting Jayda down in the pack and play gently, I walked over to my friend. "Autumn, you can't settle like that, honey," I said softly.

"You two have the men you want," Autumn retorted. "They sought after you both. I don't want you two to think I'm a loser. I get what I can and I'm okay with that."

"But we don't want to see or hear of anything bad happening to you, honey," Logan said rocking Jayden softly. "I'm sorry if I was a bit abrasive. You're like our sister. We love you. But you have to have a lot more self-love for yourself, doll. God will let the right man come to you only if you wait on God."

"Well you sure have a crazy way of showing the love!"

Autumn said smiling a little.

Storming up the hallway, Lance came to me and grabbed my arm and pulled me into the kitchen. "Excuse us, ladies," he said.

I barely had my footing as he pulled me into the kitchen. "Lance, what da hell—"

"It's Chantel! She's been taken to County Hospital! Something about a car accident," Lance said.

"Oh, my goodness!," I whispered out.

"Yes, I gotta go now," Lance replied.

"Wait, I'm going too—"

"No...you're not. Stay here with the babies. They don't need to be in that environment."

"Da hell I ain't! I'm not staying here."

"Morgan, for once will you please listen to me? I'm pretty sure everything's fine. Stay with my babies, okay? Besides, you have guests. I'll call you when I get there."

Grabbing his face, I kissed him deeply. "Please keep me posted. Tell her I love her and we'll be there later."

"I will." Lance went out the side door and took off in his truck. I walked back into the living room and sat on the couch.

"What's going on?" Logan asked.

"Chantel was in a car accident," I answered.

"What?! Oh my goodness! Why are you here? You need to get going!" Logan responded.

"I'm sorry, who's Chantel?" Autumn asked.

"Chantel is Lance's 15 year old daughter," I said.

"Logan's right, you do need to get going," Autumn agreed.

"That's what we said," Brian said walking in the living room with Mark. "He was persistent that we stayed."

"I think it'd be best if we left," Mark said to Autumn. "Maybe we can catch up before we leave Atlanta Monday morning."

"I think that's a great idea," Autumn said. "Morgan, go with your husband."

"We're *all* going," Logan said. "Get the babies, Mo. We can't leave him at the hospital like that."

"I was already thinking that, Cookie," I said. I walked over and hugged Autumn and thanked Mark for coming. We all exchanged goodnights and after Mark and Autumn left, Logan, Brian and I started gathering up the kids.

In two cars, we pulled up to the parking lot of the county hospital. After entering the hospital, I pushed the babies in their twin sitter stroller and I thanked God they were still sleeping. The whole time, I blamed myself for letting her go. I should've never let her go to the mall. I held back my tears and my anger because it was my fault that Chantel was hurt. On our way to the emergency room, I noticed Lance sitting in the waiting area with his head held low.

"Baby," I said. "What's going on? How is she?"

My husband sat silent. He finally lifted his head and said almost in a whisper, "Doctor's don't know if she's gonna make it."

## Chapter Five

We sat in the waiting room of county hospital for what seemed like an eternity waiting on Chantel's status. If that beautiful, vibrant young girl died, it would be the death of my husband...and me. As much as I wanted to break, I had to be strong for Lance. I've never seen him so somber or vulnerable. He said absolutely nothing at all. I tried to get him to talk, but sometimes silence and the physical presence is all that's needed to make a strong impact. Logan's kids were getting restless so Brian took them home. Logan told him she'd catch a ride with me later.

When Logan walked to the restroom, my husband's voice, so low and deep said, "My God. Have I not done what I was supposed to do for my daughter? In the name of Jesus, I ask that you spare her life for me. I know it's selfish, Father. I fall short every day. Whatever I'd done, please don't punish her for it. However, it's still Your will and I ask that if she's meant to leave us here on earth to get to the kingdom, then I'll have to learn to accept it."
I had both of my hands wrapped around his while he prayed out loud. For the first time ever, I saw Lance cry and it tore me up so bad that I cried too.
"I just want my baby girl to live!" Lance stated with his head low. "I can't have my life without her...without any of my children! Morgan..."
"I know, Sweetheart," I said tearfully. "I know."
With his head burrowed in my bosom, I held and comforted my husband while we continued to pray and weep for Chantel. It was at that moment I knew Lance needed to call Sharayne. Despite all the suspicious activity on her part, she was still Chantel's mother.
"Honey," I whispered into Lance's ear, "you need to call Sharayne if you haven't done so."

Lance sat up slowly and sat back in the chair with his hands over his face. Bringing his hands down finally after about ten seconds, he said, "Yeah...you're right."

He reached into his pocket for his cell phone and called her. "Hey, Sharayne. Umm...Chantel's been in a car accident and it's pretty bad....injuries are severe; doctor's think she may not make it....I—I—yes...do you think you can make it here?...No!...There's a hotel down the street from here!...Are you serious right now?!...listen, listen, I'll keep you posted until you can find a way here...we're at the County Hospital....Fulton...yeah...alright." Lance clicked off his cell phone in disgust. "You know...everyday you and I are together the more grateful I am that I finally woke up and left that female alone."

Concerned, I asked, "What happened? What did she say?"

Inhaling and exhaling sharply, Lance replied, "First, she reacted the way I expected; you know upset and everything as you and I are. Then it turned into her blaming me for this happening and her asking to stay with *us* until we know for certain what's going on with her."

I shook my head. Typical Sharayne. It made me think of the month before when we went to Charlotte for Lance's family's two day reunion they have every 3rd and 4th of July.

*************************************************

It was my first year with the family as an actual member of the family. I'd go before with A.J. and Amira when Logan asked me to go. After all, they are her late husband's children. (For those of you that have no clue, you have to read the first book in order to follow this family history) Anyway, we're all at Lance's parents' house and we stayed there for three days; all of us...Lance, myself, Keenan, Lamar, Alanna, Chantel, A.J., Amira, and the twins.

Sharayne knew we were in town and she knew that The Brooks family had a family reunion on the 3$^{rd}$ and 4$^{th}$ of July every year because she used to attend before I came into the picture. A large group of Lance's family attended. Folks from different states and throughout the city attended. Mr. Robert and Mrs. Rochelle Brooks had about an acre of backyard so it was decked out with plenty of food, music, seating, and games for the kids.

I sat next to Miss Rochelle (Lance's mom) and she was just sucking up all she could of Jayden. In her lime green sundress, her pedicure toes stood out in the lime green open toe sandals. Her short hair was dyed honey blonde and she just glowed with pride over her new grandson.

"My little man is so handsome!" Miss Rochelle exclaimed. "God knows I wanted to come down when he was born, but I had to make sure Robert was okay." Mr. Robert (Lance's dad) had hip surgery the day before the twins were born and spent four days in the hospital. So we promised to come for the family reunion. We wanted to come sooner, but I was in no shape to travel right after the babies were born.

"Miss Rochelle, we understood," I said. "Besides...they're here now and that's all that matters."

"Amen!" Miss Rochelle said. "Between you and me, Morgan, you're the best thing that's happened to my Lance. I wish you were around before he met that *thing* and had babies with her."

"Well, he tells me that also," I chimed in. "But everything was meant to happen for a reason."

"True. We don't know God's plan. But there's nothing wrong with wishful thinking."

I happened to look up and saw a sight I wished would go away instantly. "Umm, Miss Rochelle? Did anyone invite *her?"*

"Who?" Miss Rochelle asked.

I nodded toward the side entrance of the yard. It was Sharayne.

"Uh unh! I don't even know why she's here!" Miss Rochelle stated.

"I do," I said under my breath.

Sharayne walked in with a white t-shirt, jean capris, and white canvas shoes. But she didn't just walk, she sashayed in the yard. Her hair was in micros and they looked like they stunk. You could tell she needed them redone because she had so much new growth. The sun added at least another shade of darkness to her brown skin and for some reason, she looked trashier than the last time I saw her. Instead of the typical response most would expect from me, I just sat back and watched her as she made her way to Lance's sisters Teri and Finesse.

"Hmph! She raised cane when she was with my son. Being rude, disrespectful, and just didn't care about nothing that had to do with him and his wants or needs. Now that he's moved on, she keeps sniffing around here like a bloodhound," Miss Rochelle said.

"That's believable," I said.

"Well don't you worry, Morgan, I got this," Miss Rochelle stated. One thing about Miss Rochelle: she had become more spiritual in her walk with God, but there's still that part of her that's street. You know...the mother that was known for fighting any and everyone in the neighborhood growing up, not about to have anyone get over on her or her kids, and will still let the old school pop out even though she's been saved. Miss Rochelle just sat back watching like a lioness thinking of a strategy to claim her prey as she held her grandson. Sharayne sashayed her way greeting people who knew she had no business being there. Teri turned to

Sharayne with a look of disgust on her face. Teri is the same shade of honey brown like Lance. She is the youngest sister who stood at 6 feet even and used to play in the WNBA as a point guard for the Sparks. Her fire engine red dyed hair flowed down her back and it was all hers. Teri still worked out four days a week and her biceps and calf muscles were rock hard. She had a small diamond pierced in her right nostril and always wore top of the line clothing. On this particular day, she wore a soft pink Prada romper custom made for her by her designer. I had to give it to her though she had much contempt for Logan while Logan was married to her and Lance's brother Amari. Teri turned to Sharayne face-to-face and said, "What da hell you doin' here?"

"It's the family reunion and I wanna see my kids," replied Sharayne.

"Umm...key word is *family*. You're not a part of this family, Boo-Boo," Teri snarled back.

"Well, I beg to differ," Sharayne snapped back. "I vested four kids and well over ten years with y'all."

"Look here, cow, you ain't welcomed here! Now you wanna pop up because my big brother moved on without yo' stankin' ass?! For what?! He got his queen!"

"Psh, whatever, *Teri*! Ya needs ta move and let me go holla at my kids!"

"Those half-grown people you call kids don't even want you around...especially after that stunt you pulled a while back. Oh we haven't forgotten and I still owe you for lettin' that bastard try to rape my niece!" At that point, Teri was so close to Sharayne's face she could've kissed her on the forehead. Mr. Robert walked over and stood between the two women.

"Sharayne," he said in his fatherly tone, "you know you're not welcomed here. Why do you do this?"

"Mr. Rob, as long as my kids are here, so am I," she replied.

"Now, I see them over there playing volleyball. Let me just say my hello and I'll be gone. I promise."

Hesitating, Mr. Robert looked at Sharayne with his hazel green eyes and white hair and said, "Okay. You have ten minutes. But you need to set up a time and place for them to come and see you. All of this popping up now after you didn't want to be a part of my son's life and using them as bargaining chips isn't working. Besides...the boys aren't even boys anymore and your girls are another story.

Teri...honey...come on, now."

Mr. Robert always had a way with Teri. After all, she was his baby girl biologically and his only child period. He loved Finesse, Amari, and Lance like his own and never showed division or favoritism because of DNA and I can see how Miss Rochelle loved him for that as well as Lance and Finesse. Amari used to tell Logan how much he wished he knew more about his biological father though they had met. But he knew Mr. Robert as his dad and that's all that mattered to him.

Sharayne walked over to Keenan, Lamar, Alanna, and Chantel who were playing against Finesse's children, their cousins, in volleyball. Chantel and Alanna looked as if they'd seen something from hell. Keenan and Lamar just stood back.

"Well, aren't y'all happy to see me?" Sharayne asked forcing hugs on her children.

"Sup, Ma," Keenan replied. His body towered over his mother's as he reached down to give her a hug. Keenan stayed in the gym and worked his body out to the max. His arms, shoulders, neck, and chest was so swollen with muscles he looked like a young Michael Jai White.

"Look at you, Keenan!" Sharayne exclaimed. "College is doing you some good! And Lamar...you're just as handsome as your father!"

"Thank you, Ma," Lamar said reaching to give his mother a hug. Lamar had a growth spurt during his senior year of high school just before he went off to college and grew to 6 feet 1 inch tall...just like Lance. "Umm...what are you doing here?"

"Lamar, that wasn't very nice," Sharayne quipped.

"I'm just saying...this is weird," Lamar said.

"Very," Chantel added.

Sharayne turned to her daughters. She had to have felt the ice coming from their eyes. "Well, hello girls."

Alanna hesitantly said, "Hi. How are you?"

"Too good to give me a hug? Both of you?" Sharayne questioned.

"I'm good," Alanna said. "I'd just rather not front like we're all Kool and The Gang when we're not."

"Little girl, don't go there with me," Sharayne snapped. "I'm still your mother and I have right to see you if I want to."

"Well, what if we don't want you here?" Alanna asked.

"Remember, you chose that—that man over us!" Chantel snapped.

"I did no...such...thing!" Sharayne declared.

"Ma...I think you better leave," Keenan said softly. "This ain't the time nor place."

"Oh..you sidin' with them?" Sharayne said to Keenan. At this point, Lance was high-tailing it to his young adults. I was right behind him and so was Miss Rochelle still holding my son. Teri was coming with Finesse as Finesse held my daughter. Realizing that there was a gang of Brooks' coming up behind her, Sharayne turned around with her eyes as wide as a deer in headlights.

Lance stood two arms length back away from Sharayne but looked at her head on.

"Sharayne, you've had your time here to see them or talk to them or whatever," he said. "If they wanna spend time with you or see you before they leave, they will on their time. Right now, I'm asking you...politely...to leave."

Surveying the people around her and stopping to size me up and down, she said, "Okay. I don't want any trouble from y'all. I just wanted to see my kids since you won't let me see them, Lance."

"This ain't the time, Ray," Lance said assertively. "Go and go now."

Without any words, Sharayne turned to her kids one last time hoping they'd say something to support her. When they didn't, she turned around and slowly started walking. Sharayne fixated her eyes on me and walked passed me sizing me up and down as she walked by me with a smirk on her face. Lance grabbed my wrist and pulled me close to him so he could put his arm around my waist and keep me from the temptation of punching her in the mouth. I knew one day we were going to cross paths and I really wish I didn't have that gut feeling because I'm usually on point when I do feel that way.

Miss Rochelle and Finesse walked back to the patio to sit down with Jayda and Jayden. Teri walked over to the drink table and Lance and I talked to Keenan, Lamar, Alanna, and Chantel. Like a king checking on his court, Lance asked, "Is everyone good?"

"Yeah, Dad," they all said simultaneously.

He wasn't buying it from Chantel or Alanna. "Girls?"

"I can't believe her!" Alanna stated. "Why would she come *here* of all places?"

Keenan chimed in, "Because she had a grain of hope thinking some of us would feel sorry for her and give her the opportunity to see us. But I'm a grown ass man. I'll see her if I want to or not."

Lamar said his peace, "Man, regardless she's still our

mother. Maybe we ought to give her a chance; hear her out."

"Damn that!" Chantel exclaimed. "She blamed me for Pete coming on to me and she still stayed with that dude!"

"Naw, Sis," Lamar cut in. "Dude got picked up for raping some little girl three months ago. Ma ain't with him no more."

"So?! She stayed with him up until them, right?" Keenan said. "Bottom line is she didn't support our sisters and she stayed with a pedophile until he was caught. Mother or not, she was foul."

Lamar looked at his brother and said, "That's why we need to hear her out."

"Lamar, I know you're all into the Lord and that's a beautiful thing, but I can't say I'm forgiving her for that," Keenan replied.

Lance and I stood back and listened to them. He finally said, "Hey...listen...we're all affected by what happened. I did everything I could to keep myself from going to jail...trust me. Right now, let's get back to having fun and not letting a hiccup interrupt our time, okay? And that's your mother...you can see her or seek her whenever you want to. Just because things didn't work out between us doesn't mean you have to side with me or her. No matter how I feel about her or anyone else on that side of your family. Got me?"

All four nodded their heads in agreement. "Cool," Lance said. "Now get back to your game. Looks like y'all losing anyway." Keenan, Lamar, Alanna, and Chantel waved us off and got back to playing against their cousins. Still with his arm around my waist, Lance and I were in step with each other walking back to our babies who were now held by Mr. Robert and Teri.

"Hey, Mo," Teri started, "where's the diaper bag? It smells

like Jayda needs her little butt changed."

"Oh that's right. We went to the store earlier and I left it in the car," I answered. "I'll be right back."

I walked around the side of the house to get to Miss Rochelle's car that we drove earlier to Kroger's. I still had her keys in my back pocket of my purple shorts and was about to pull them out when I noticed Sharayne was hanging around the 10-passenger rental van of Lance and I's. Cautiously I walked over to her and asked, "What's the problem?"

"Nice van," she said not answering me. "Must've set y'all back a pretty penny."

"Why are you still here, Sharayne?" I asked.

"Question is why are you still here?" she sarcastically asked back.

"Excuse me?"

"You heard me. Don't you see what's going on? Lance is only using you to get me back."

"What?!"

"Oh, yeah. Marrying you...taking my kids...all just a ploy to make me realize how stupid I was for not marrying him when he asked me years ago. All I gotta do is get him alone, talk to him softly like he likes, rub on that hard and chiseled chest, and let everything take place."

I felt fire in the pit of my stomach and my fingers balled into a fist down at my sides. I was telling myself to calm down because I didn't want to ruin my husband's family day. Still talking, Sharayne said, "You know all of those wonderful moves he made with you to have your babies in the bedroom? He learned all of that from me teaching him. So while you're enjoying him mount on your aggressively, yet ever so gently, keep this in mind: *I taught him.* Even how to do the butterfly kiss on the second pair of lips you have." At that moment, I saw nothing but my closed fist connecting to her face and rage surfacing with every blow I threw. Sharayne connected a punch to my chest as she tried to punch me in my face. I went to grab for her neck but she ducked and grabbed me around my waist trying to slam me to the ground. I had to give it to her...she was a fighter. I extended my legs out and locked my knees so she couldn't move me and I dropped an elbow into her spine two times as hard as I could which made her let me go. I connected a right fist into her jaw and she hit the grass. I tried to stomp her face with my foot but she rolled out of the way. Before she could go anywhere else, I grabbed her smelly micro braids with my left hand, wrapped as much as I could around my hand and punched her repetitively in her face until my hand was wet with her blood. Then, I felt something inside of me that I never felt before and as that rage surged through me, I let go of her hair and positioned my hands on the sides of her head ready to snap her neck.

"Morgan! No!" yelled Miss Rochelle. "Lance! Somebody! Stop her!" I instantly stopped myself from killing Sharayne as her bloody face looked up at me. I felt my body being yanked from over Sharayne by Lance. He put me behind him and kept a hold of me to make sure I was guarded by him. Sharayne slowly got up spitting out a mouth full of blood.

"Get the hell outta here, Ray!" Lance bellowed. "Now!"

Panting heavily, Sharayne said, "This ain't over yet, bitch! Remember...I taught him all of that! Those are my kids! You just the jump off!"

"Yo, let me get her!" Teri said handing Jayda back to Finesse.

"No, ain't nobody getting nobody!" Mr. Robert said. "Sharayne take your ass home now!"

By this time, mostly everyone in Lance's family gathered to the front of the house to see what was going on. Sharayne got into her yellow Pontiac Sunbird and pathetically drove away.

We stood on the front lawn and watched her drive off until she was out of sight. Lance's family walked back around the back...all except his children, Miss Rochelle, and Teri who circled around me.

"Mo, what happened? How did y'all end up fighting? Lance asked.

"I came out here to get Jayda's diaper bag and noticed her walking around our van. I asked her what was going on and she started saying dumb stuff to me," I answered.

"Mo-Ma..." Chantel said crying.

"Aww, Chantel, I'm sorry," I apologized.

"How could you do that?" Alanna asked me.

Taken aback I said, "Alanna, I never had any intentions of fighting with your mother. Despite my discontent with her, I still never wanted to do that."

Shaking her head implying disagreement, Alanna walked away with Keenan right behind her.

"Chantel...Lamar...I swear to both of you I never intended to do this with your mother," I said.

"Mo-Ma," Lamar began, "I believe you. But I think it's going to take a lot more to convince Alanna." He and Chantel gave me a hug and walked back to the yard. Teri and Miss Rochelle gave me a hug also, got Jayda's diaper bag, and walked back to the yard. Lance and I stayed out front for a while.

"Mo..." Lance started.

"Baby, not now...please," I said.

"I know you two will never get along, but..."

"...No, Lance, you weren't out here when she insulted me! Now, I've been keeping a lid on my temper but she crossed the line! I don't wanna talk about this anymore. I just wanna

get cleaned up and go back to having fun, okay?"
Softly, he said, "Okay, baby. C'mon...let me help you."
We walked in through the front door of Lance's parents'
house and up to the room we slept in during our stay. I
pulled out my white strapless jumpsuit and lay it on the bed.
Lance came into the bedroom with a wet, soapy washcloth
to clean off my face, neck, and hands. The look of distress
was all over Lance's face as I allowed him to clean me up.
"Mo, honey, I love you and only you. You're the woman who
won my heart, mind, and soul. I don't care what she said to
you because it was a bunch of bull. You're who I dream
about, who I long for, and who I give my all to. It's only you
and always will be you." He put the washcloth down on the
dresser and put his hands on the sides of my face. "I love
you Morgan."
"I love you too, Lance."
His lips connected with mine very deeply and sensually. His
hands left my face and ended up on my hips and around the
small of my back. He forced his tongue into my mouth and I
felt a surge of urgency come from his kiss and I was totally
lost. Then the words Sharayne belted from her mouth
popped up in my head and I pushed my husband back. I
looked into his eyes and wanted to ask him if what she said
was true. Then I thought about that and thought it would be
a bit hypocritical considering I learned some things from the
men in my past and I had no reason to be jealous or
insecure because I had Lance now. He was my husband
now and I vowed to love him no matter what.
*****************************************************

"Mr. Brooks?" a voice called from the nurse's
station. Lance, Logan, and I stood up and walked over to
the counter.
"I'm going to take you back to see your daughter now," the

nurse who was working with Chantel's doctor declared. Logan said she'd stay in the waiting area with the twins. We followed Chantel's nurse back to her room. When we entered the corridor to Chantel's room, I instantly felt sick to my stomach. I saw the curvy young girl lying in the hospital bed almost lifeless. Two doctors and another nurse were by her bedside. Lance and I just stood there looking at what was in front of us. One of the doctors walked over to us. His thin and pale body took long strides and introduced himself to us.

"Hi, I'm Dr. Ferguson, one of the surgeons who will be working on your daughter," he said.

"I'm Lance Brooks and this is my wife, Morgan, and her sister Logan" Lance said. "What's going on with our daughter?"

"We were able to stabilize Chantel before we move her into surgery. She has a broken blood vessel under her skull and part of her lower lumbar vertebrae has been dislocated. All of this is very risky and could cost her life."

Keeping his composure, Lance said, "Do whatever you have to do to save my daughter. Whatever it takes."

The other surgeon walked over to us and introduced himself as well. He told us it was time to get Chantel into surgery at that very moment. As she was being rolled out of the room and into surgery, Lance stopped the escort and kissed Chantel on her swollen face. "Telly, we're not leaving you. We love you." Lance backed up and let the escorts take her to surgery. I put my hands around my husband to comfort and support him. He held me tightly and I felt my strong husband's body sink to the floor with me still in his grasp. Lance completely fell apart and I didn't know how to deal with this. "Honey, Lance, you have to be strong and you have to pray, Baby," I said with tears streaming down my face. Lance let out this painful cry that I've never heard and it scared me. *God, please don't take Chantel away from this man or this family*, I prayed. Though accidents happen every day, I blamed myself for this. I let her go off with her friends after I was hesitant on doing so. If this child dies, what am I going to do? How can I face my husband? How am I going to be there for him?

Five hours had passed and we were all in the waiting area. Lance was pacing, Logan was sleeping curled up on a chair, and I was holding Jayda who was very bright eyed and wanting me to talk to her. It's like she understood everything that was going on and she listened to me without anything more than some coos and smiles. Of course she had to eat and was getting just as big as her brother. Then...Dr. Ferguson entered the waiting area.

"Mr. and Mrs. Brooks, hello again," he announced. Logan sat straight up as if she weren't sleeping at all. Lance walked over to the doctor who stood next to where I sat.

"How is she?" Lance asked frantically.

Scratching his head, Dr. Ferguson said, "I must say she has to have angels watching over her because Chantel's going to be alright."

"Praise Jesus!" Lance yelled. "Thank you God!"

"Amen!" shouted Logan.

"Now with the extent of head trauma she has, Chantel will have to go through rehabilitation therapy upon her discharge," Dr. Ferguson informed. "She will have to remain here until we are comfortable and certain that she will be able to go home."

"Absolutely," Lance said. "Can we go see her now?"

"Give us about ten minutes before you do so," Dr. Ferguson said. "She's still coming out of recovery and will be transferred to her room. I'll make sure one of the nurses take you to her."

"Thank you, Dr. Ferguson," Lance said.

"No problem. I'll see you all soon," the doctor replied.

"Lord Jesus," Logan said. "The power of prayer is real as it can get."

"That's true," I agreed. "So very true."

Lance pulled out his cell phone and began dialing. I was going to ask who he was calling but I knew he was calling his mother first. Anytime anything goes on major, he calls her first.

"Mom...she's gonna be alright!" Lance said in the phone as he walked toward the corridor of the waiting room. Logan sent a text message to Brian and I called Keenan and Lamar to update them and I tried calling Alanna but she never picked up. So I sent her a text message. However, as soon as I hit send, she and Shakim were walking in the waiting room.

"Dad! Mo-Ma!" Alanna exclaimed. "What...what happened? Where is she?"

Lance walked over to them and hugged a shaken Alanna. "She was in a car accident," Lance answered. "But she came out of surgery and the doctor said she'll be fine."

Alanna started bawling uncontrollably and her father held onto her as if he were protecting her from the boogeyman. Shakim stood by the door trying not to make eye contact with me.

"How ya doin', Mr. Brooks?" Shakim asked Lance.

"Could be better, young man," Lance responded. "Thank you for bringing Alanna here."

"No doubt," Shakim said. "I know how much she loves her sister and this family. It's all she talks about."

I put Jayda in the stroller, buckled her in securely, and walked over to Alanna. I needed her to know I would always be there for her despite any conflict that may arise between us.

"Lanna," I said putting my hand on her shoulder. She turned and looked at me after letting go of her father and fell into my bosom bawling.

"I'm so sorry, Mo-Ma," she said crying. Lance looked at me confused as if to say *sorry about what.*

"It's not your fault," I whispered to her as I was slowly escorting her away from her father so she wouldn't say anything else to incriminate herself and have him suspicious. "Mo-Ma, I love y'all...all of y'all...and..."

"Don't, Alanna. I know. It's okay. I love you very much and you know that. No matter what goes on with us, I love you all."

"Brooks Family?" a nurse announced and we all turned toward the short, round woman dressed in nurse scrubs. "Please follow me. I'm going to take you all to Chantel's room."

Doing as she said, Lance, Logan, Alanna, Shakim, the twins, and I followed the nurse to Chantel's room. What took five minutes felt like fifty minutes from walking down the hall to an elevator that took us to the 3$^{rd}$ floor toward the ICU wing. "Now, only two visitors are allowed to go in at a time," the nurse reported. "There's the waiting room there. We ask that you scrub up and wash your hands before entering her room."

"Mo, you and I will go first," Lance instructed. Everyone else nodded in agreement. While the others sat in the ICU waiting area, Lance and I walked to her room. We picked up the scrubs that were in the pockets of the door rack outside of her room and put them on ourselves. When we walked in her room, we both stopped at the sink and began washing our hands. I felt my stomach do flops and I wasn't familiar with that feeling. Lance walked toward her first and I followed. Chantel was on a ventilator and was hooked up to so many monitors. Lance placed his hands over one of hers.

"Telly, it's me, Dad," Lance whispered. "I'm here, princess. So is Morgan. Alanna, Logan, the twins...they're all here to see you. I promise you I'll stay right here by your side. The doctor said you'll be fine and you're gonna pull through. You just have to do your part and make it happen." I've seen my husband in so many different lights. Seeing him this open and vulnerable is so new for me and in all honesty, I didn't know how to take it. I didn't see him as less of a man because he wept over his daughter. I saw him as a man who had feelings and heart and enough strength to show he also have weakness too. Lance leaned down to kiss Chantel on the forehead and started to stroke her arm. I kept trying to not blame myself for this. I knew how much Lance didn't like one young man in question that Chantel was going to hang out with. Which dawned on me....where were the other families? I'm pretty sure GBI investigated this and I know Lance all too well to know he was going to be up on this.

Chantel's face was swollen and she had her head wrapped with bandages. The tube going down her throat was annoying to see and she looked almost lifeless. All of this because I told her to go somewhere without talking to her father first. Some step-mother I was. I stepped away from her and Lance and was about to go to the waiting area to allow Alanna to come in when Lance asked, "Where are you going, Mo?"

"I'm going to let Alanna come in," I answered. He nodded and I walked out taking off the hospital gear and tossing it in the trash can. As I crossed the hall to get to the waiting area, I noticed two uniformed policemen standing in there as well as four other young people and three other adults who I knew nothing about. Logan noticed me and stood up next to the twins. As I entered, Logan and Alanna had looks of urgency on their faces.

"What's going on?" I asked. The two policemen turned to me. I recognized them as they work for my husband on extreme cases.

"Hey, Morgan," Officer Broadus said. He was a very stout man who had a clean shaven face and a very deep voice.

"Hello, Morgan," Officer Adams said. He was tall and slim and was the office motor mouth and a foul mouth Lance couldn't stand.

"Morgan, could we speak with you privately?" Officer Broadus asked.

"Just one second," I said. "Who are you all?" I asked the four other people in the waiting area.

"I—I—I'm Octavia's sister, Mrs. Brooks...I'm Olivia," announced one very thin light-skinned girl.

"I'm Jamelle," answered a dark-skinned boy all of a good 130 pounds at five foot six.

"I'm DeMarcus," replied another dark-skinned boy around 170 at about the same height as Jamelle.

"I'm Tramarvious," stated the other brown-skinned boy who stood at five ten about 170 also. So...this is the one Chantel was head over heads for. He was a young cutie; I'd give her that. His dreadlocks were neatly maintained on his shoulders and he had full grown beard. But his whole aura reeked of uncertainty. I looked at Olivia and asked, "How's your sister?"

"We don't know yet. She's still in surgery," Olivia answered. "My mom's still waiting to hear something. Octavia has been in surgery for a long time now. I wanted to come up and see what's going on with Chantel before I go back downstairs."

"Well right now it's looking hopeful," I said. "Tell your mom I'll be down soon to see her, okay?"

"Yes, ma'am," Olivia said. Officer Broadus interrupted with,

"Morgan? Are you ready?"

"Yes," I answered. We walked out into the hallway and Logan was right with me.

"Ma'am, this doesn't pertain to you," Officer Adams snarled at Logan.

"Shut up, Adams. This is my sister and she has the right to know also," I snapped back.

Officer Broadus cleared his throat. "Morgan, your husband is going to flip his lid when he finds out what was going on. Apparently, your daughter, Olivia, and Octavia were all headed to North Point Mall. They had marijuana and alcohol in the car. Octavia was driving...and she was high off of weed and driving at a very high speed. Octavia went through a red light and was caught by one of the patrolmen on duty. He tried to pull them over, but Octavia started to flee."

"Oh...no!" I said.

"Yes," Officer Adams said. "It gets worse."

"How much worse can this get?" Logan questioned.

"Well, the chase went on for about ten minutes until Octavia lost control of the car," Officer Adams added. "She spun out of control and ended up in an embankment off of the highway. Chantel was thrown from the vehicle and was found about a yard away from the car. Olivia and Octavia were pinned in the car though the airbags were deployed."

"However, the only person buckled in the seatbelt was Olivia," Officer Broadus added.

"So, now what?" I asked.

"Now we face your husband," Officer Adams said.

"Mo, once Lance finds out Chantel was probably drinking and/or smoking, he's going to flip," Logan said.

"I know...I know," I stated.

"What am I going to flip out about?" Lance asked startling me as he walked into the hallway. "Adams...Broadus...what did you find out?"

Both officers looked at each other, then me, and started telling Lance the exact same story they told me. Lance stood with his arms crossed looking down at the floor as the other two men explained the situation that took place. My husband stood there shaking his head for a while letting all of the information sink in. He then looked up and through the door of the waiting room where he noticed Chantel's friends. He pointed to Olivia and gestured her to come out to the hallway. Scared, Olivia walked out to the hallway with us.

"Yes, sir?" Olivia peeped.

"How old are you now, Olivia?" Lance asked.

"I'm 16, Sir," she answered.

"Did you know your sister was high?" Lance asked.

"Y—yes sir," Olivia answered.

"Have you been drinking or smoking?" Lance asked.

"N—no sir," Olivia answered.

"Do you often ride with your sister when she's under the influence?" Lance questioned again.

"Not often, sir," she replied.

"Was my daughter drinking or smoking?" he asked again.

Hesitantly, Olivia answered, "Yes, Sir. She was drinking, but not smoking."

"What about you? Were you drinking or smoking?" he asked.

"No, Sir," Olivia answered.

"That's true, Brooks," Officer Broadus said. "We got that result from the doctor after we requested a blood toxicity test on all three of them. Your daughter did have a blood alcohol reading that was just under the legal amount for someone her size, though she's underage. But it didn't show any traces of THC."

"Your mother's downstairs, right?" Lance asked Olivia.

"Yes, sir. She's waiting for Octavia to come out of surgery," she answered.

"Miss Clements is aware of everything as well," Officer Adams said. Miss Clements is Octavia and Olivia's mother.

"Good. I want to go see her," Lance said.

"I'm coming with you," I said.

"Mo...Lance...how about I take the twins back home? I'll meet you at your house whenever you get there. It's really late and they don't need to be here all night," Logan suggested.

"How about you and Mo go back home?" Lance said handing me his keys. "I'm staying here. There's some things I need to find out with Miss Clements and with those boys in there."

"Baby—" I started.

"—Mo, go home with our babies. I'll keep you posted, okay?"

I did what my husband suggested. I gave him a kiss and started pushing the babies down the hall to the elevator as they were reclined in their stroller. This was going to be a long night and the first night since we were married that I was going to be sleeping alone.

Logan and I arrived back at my house thirty minutes later. We took the babies out of their car seats and got them situated for the night once we got into the house. I was so tired and I didn't recognize it until I got ready to shower. I went into the master bathroom and turned the shower on. I got into the steady stream of cool water that filtered through the shower head. It was too humid to take a hot or warm shower and it was very relaxing to me and much needed. After lathering and rinsing and drying, I got my night clothes out for the evening. Logan knocked on the bedroom door before entering.

"Hey, Mo, I just talked to Brian. He told me he can handle the kids for the night and suggested I stay with you."

"Cookie, you don't have to stay. I'll be alright with the babies. And Lance will keep me posted with any and everything going on."

"Mo, you know I'm not leaving your side. We're family through thick and thin."

"Thank you, Cookie." I walked over to climb into my wonderfully comfortable king size bed and Logan sprawled out on the foot of the bed. I think she drifted right off to sleep in no time while I pondered around with my television remote control to find something to watch on our wall mounted 64" flat screen. I found some reruns of The Cosby Show and started to drift off to sleep. However, I was awakened by my cell phone. I reached over to the nightstand and picked it up. It was Lance.

"Hey, Sweetie," I answered. "What's going on?"

"A whole lot of mess," he spoke through the receiver of his phone. "I had a long talk with Chantel's guy friends; especially Tramarvious. I told her I didn't want her hanging around him and I made sure he heard it from me face to face in front of witnesses. But things didn't turn out too well for Olivia's family....Octavia died."

"Oh, no!" I said sitting straight up in the bed.

"Yes. There was too much internal bleeding and she had too many other injuries to name. I went down to give my condolences to her mom and Olivia. Mo...we should've prayed for Octavia too. I feel a little guilty that we were too selfish to pray for that girl."

"Sweetie...the only thing we can do now is pray for her soul and for her family. I'll make sure I go see Olivia and her mother, Dawna, tomorrow."

After I hung up with Lance, I felt so bad that Chantel's best friend passed and she didn't even know it. I know my husband well enough to know he's already planning how we're going to be a part of this...

## Chapter Six

October 2009. It had been two months since Octavia Clements' funeral. Chantel is home now and still undergoing rehabilitation and is still mourning over Octavia. Lance was right there with her through everything; when she was taken off of the ventilator and all. Sharayne did come the next day of Chantel being in the hospital and was actually doing a wonderful job not thinking about herself for a change. Keenan and Lamar came home every weekend to see her for the three weeks Chantel was hospitalized. The babies and I came every evening after I got off from work and picked them up from day care. Alanna was there every day after school. The only time he wasn't in the room is when he had to come home to shower or when she was getting bathed by the CNA.

On the day Chantel woke up, Lance was beside himself and it was two days before Octavia's funeral. He and Sharayne sat at her bedside and were joyous to see their daughter waking. I would've been there myself, but Chantel woke up during the time I was at work. After the doctors and nurses checked over Chantel's vitals and tests, they were pleased with the results and shared their optimism of a good recovery with Lance and Sharayne. Once they left the room, Chantel hoarsely and softly said, "Dad...Dad..."
"Yes, Telly, I'm here," he responded.
"Where am I?" she asked still with her eyes closed and head bandaged.
"Princess, you're in the hospital. You were in a car accident."
"Where's...Octavia...Olivia...they were...with me?"
"Chantel, it's Mommy," Sharayne quietly announced. "You don't need to worry about that right now."
"Dad...where's...Mo-Ma? Where's...Octavia?"
"Telly, Morgan is at work. She'll be here later," Lance

answered.

"Octavia? Where is...she?"

Lance danced around that as long as he could. He tried to find the right words and said, "Honey...Octavia is resting peacefully. We'll talk about that later." He couldn't bring himself to tell Chantel that her best friend died as she was coming out of her coma. Just he telling her Octavia was resting seemed to calm her down and she kept quiet for a little while.

The day of the funeral, Lance and I went to pay our respects to the Clements family. I don't care what I may feel about anyone's children, I'd never wish or pray death upon them. Dawna Clements held up the best she could during the funeral until the casket closed on her daughter. She, Olivia, and other relatives and schoolmates were there and not a dry eye was in the building. I remember whispering to Lance how much I can't bear to be there because it hurt to be a part of this. He reminded me not only were we there to show our support to Dawna, but for Chantel as well who couldn't be there. Needless to say, the day before the funeral Sharayne distastefully told a still fragile Chantel that her best friend died. That sent Chantel off in a tailspin and Lance was not happy at all.

Chantel was home from her rehab session in October and was still learning how to walk again. Graduating from a wheelchair to a walker, Chantel posted up in her bedroom after deep physical and occupational therapy. I went to her room to check on her and she was positioning the walker next to her bed.

"Hey...let me help you," I offered.

"Mo-Ma, I'm okay," Chantel grunted climbing into bed. "Gia the therapist said to try and maneuver as much as I could."

"Yes, but she didn't tell you to reject assistance, did she?"

Laughing, Chantel said, "No." I walked over to Chantel and helped her get into her bed. I positioned her legs on the bed to make sure she was comfortable. She had her back against her headboard with extra pillows for support. Because of the skull procedure, a portion of Chantel's hair was shaven and you could see where the incision was. To cover it, Chantel wore a short hair-styled wig resembling her natural hair whenever she went outside of the house. She was determined to walk again, dance again, and be herself again. She was aware that she would never be 100% due to her spinal injury, but she was determined to try and get there. Olivia and some other girls from her school came to visit often; even DeMarcus and Jamelle. Tramarvious tried, but Lance just wasn't feeling it. So he often would send gifts, letters, and money to Chantel via Olivia or Jamelle. I knew about it; I just didn't say anything to Lance. I had a chance to talk to Tramarvious and throughout all of the trouble he used to get himself into, he's trying to do right by Chantel and win Lance's approval someday.

"I still can hear her laughter, Mo-Ma," Chantel expressed. "I can hear her jokes, her voice...I can still see her as if she were here."
"You'll always have that, Chantel," I replied. "There's nothing like good memories to take away from any hurt that goes on."
"I'll tell you one thing, Mo-Ma...I'm never drinking again...ever."
"What possessed y'all to do that anyway?"
"Well...we've done it before."
"What?!"
"I know...I know...we were being stupid, foolish..."
"And downright crazy! You have any idea what your father would do, or would have done, had he known y'all had been

doing this before?"

"Yes, ma'am."

"And you know how you feel right now at this very moment about Octavia not being here? How do you think we would be right now if it was you alongside her in the grave? Honey, with every action there's a reaction and a consequence. Trust me...I am notorious for doing dumb stuff. But the important thing is for you to know what not to do and to do what you need to in school. You're going to be a very successful person; I know it."

"Thank you, Mo-Ma."

I gave Chantel a hug and walked out of her room pulling it up a little to give her a sense of privacy. I refused to close it all of the way because if she needed something, anyone in the house needed to be able to hear her ask for help.

\*\*\*\*\*\*\*\*\*\*\*\*\*\*\*\*\*\*\*\*\*\*\*\*\*\*\*\*\*\*\*\*\*\*\*\*\*\*\*\*\*\*\*\*\*\*\*\*\*\*

Since Alanna was at work, I asked Logan to keep an eye on the babies while I went to my kickboxing class. I was determined to lose this baby weight if it killed me. After dropping the babies off with Logan and Brian, I went to my class three miles from their home in downtown Alpharetta. It was my third night and it felt good getting some cardio and strengthening done. Grant it I could do my own, I needed another outlet besides my husband and sister. I really didn't have any friends besides Autumn, who went back to Texas after her meeting with Kevin Littleton. When I arrived into the building, I threw my small duffel-like bag on the floor next to the wall mirror in the back of the studio. I already had on my Nike athletic wear and shoes and I began to stretch. One young woman there, named Naomi, had been a professional MMA fighter for five years and was one of the instructors there for the last two years. She knew her stuff and had no problem teaching the women how to defend themselves. She was about 5'4" with long, blonde hair and dark green eyes. Naomi was very muscular, but not mannish. As she was prepping up for the class, she had all of us gather around.

"Ladies and gentlemen! Listen up! As much as I don't like to announce this, I have to inform you all that my partner, Joe, will no longer be here due to unforeseen circumstances with his family. He had to move back to California and on behalf of everyone here, I wished him the best."

Everyone in the room murmured amongst each other.

"However...I won't be the only instructor as I know that some of you men in here aren't too keen on women instructors! So...it is my pleasure to introduce to you my new partner who will be here on a part time basis...Mr. Victor Diez!"

*Victor Diez?! This can't be...this...can't...be!*

Amongst all of the applauding, Victor walked from a side door of the kickboxing studio. It was him! Smiling that same smile that blew me away in college and with a very faint scar on his face from where I cut him. He took long strides to the center of the floor and while he did, I inched to the back of the class and tried to hide behind two of the tallest men there only with enough eyesight to see Victor from a distance. He stood there in a black tank top, black and white boxing training shorts and no shoes or socks. He was still had that dark hair and icy blue eyes that apparently still made women woo over him. I heard a couple of women make comments on how good he looked and how they hope to get one-on-one instruction as he spoke. The Cuban-Italian man told about his accolades and what he did for a living and then wanted everyone to introduce themselves....*oh no!* Of the twenty-five students, including myself, 12 were men. I kept my head down so my dreadlocks were hanging in front of my face while everyone called introduced themselves. Finally, I hear Naomi say, "Hey, Morgan, are you okay?" I slowly raised my head and said, "Yes."

"Good, you had me scared there for a moment," she said. When I finally connected eyes with Victor, his facial expression went from shock to surprise.

"Morgan? Morgan Chambers...is that *you*?" Victor asked walking toward me. Everyone looked at me as if there were a spotlight in the room. I just nodded my head, forced a smile and said, "Hello, Victor. Long time."

"Indeed," Victor said. "Ladies and gentlemen, this young lady here is the reason I got into kickboxing. She broke my heart back in college." Everyone awed at his response. But little did they know he was probably dead serious. "Well, it's nice to meet everyone and I hope we all have some serious fun tonight! Let's pair up with some warm ups and stretches!"

Naomi and Victor walked around the studio coaching and cheering on the other kickboxing attendees. I was paired up with a lady named Jamie who was a wife of a baseball player for the Atlanta Braves. We took turns hitting and kicking the punching bag as instructed alternating hits and kicks. Then I felt two very familiar hands on my biceps trying to guide my throws into the body bag and it sent bad chills up and down my spine. Victor was very sweaty and the heat rolled off of him as if he were on fire. Softly, he said to me, "You want to make your jabs connect quickly and with enough force that will not dislocate your shoulder, crack your knuckles, or sprain your wrists."

I kept my focus on the punching bag and done what I was instructed with Naomi two nights before. However, to entertain Victor, I added some of his suggestions to my workout.

"Looking good, Morgan," he said slyly as he walked away

from me and on to the next attendee. I couldn't believe he was here...of all of the places in the world...here.

At the end of class, I didn't bother to shower as planned. I grabbed my bag and dashed out to my Durango. As I was clicking the unlock button from my key remote, out comes Victor.

"You just gonna run out like that?" Victor asked rhetorically. I kept walking to my car not saying a word. I wasn't afraid of him...I was afraid of myself.

"Morgan...c'mon...I just—"

"—You just what, Victor?!" I spun around asking.

"I just wanted to catch up with you that's all...see what you've been up to since '99...how'd you end up here...you know...catch up." Victor stood in front of me at arm's length. He was even more attractive now than he was back in college. But I still didn't forget that this guy raped me though I got up and got him for the hurt he inflicted upon me.

"We have nothing to talk about, Victor. Nothing to catch up on...nothing."

"Morgan, you've been on my mind for ten years. I've tried everything to contact you or to find you. I just wanted to apologize...that's all. I was a jerk and...I definitely deserved that ass whoopin'."

"I don't believe you."

He took a step close to me and I stepped back. "Morgan, I truly am sorry. I was caught up into myself and...I should've never done that to you. Please...let me make it up to you." I kept looking at him trying to feel him out. One thing about Victor that I did learn was that he was good at conning people and making them take his word on a lot of b.s.

"Yeah...you shouldn't have done that to me...or any other female for that matter."

"Morgan, I had nothing but bad luck since. Besides, your stab marks are stuck with me like old luggage. Please accept my apology. I'm asking for forgiveness and I promise you I'll leave you alone."

God, why do we have to forgive a person who asks for forgiveness?

"Okay...I'll accept your apology and forgive you. Just know this...I'll never forget...and my husband is a GBI officer." I opened the door of my Durango and climbed in. Standing outside of the studio, Victor waved until I pulled off.

As I was in route to Logan and Brian's house, I called Autumn on my cell phone. *Please answer the phone*, I thought. On the fifth ring, she answered.

"Hey girl!" Autumn screeched into the phone. "What's going on?"

"You're not going to believe who my new kickboxing instructor is....Victor Diez."

"*What?!*" Autumn yelled. "Are you serious right now?"

"Have I ever not kept it 100 with you?"

"Girl...whatchu gonna do? Are you dropping the class? Are you gonna tell your husband?"

"It would look really suspicious to Lance that I'd drop a class he suggested for me to take that he knew I'd enjoy."

"Well, you gotta do something. You know you have moments of reckless behavior."

"Not recently I haven't. I've never let anyone run me away and I'm not about to have Victor run me off either."

"Good. Just be careful. Anyway, my brother and I are on our way to the Jazzfest. Keep me posted, okay?"

"Yeah, I will." I hung up my cell phone and made it to Logan and Brian's house. A.J., Aleasha, Amira, and Austin were all out in the yard playing. Brian and Logan were sitting on the porch watching while holding Jayda and Jayden. I walked to their porch and was greeted with two five month olds who were flapping their arms when they noticed me with excitement.

"How was class?" Logan asked.

"It was good," I said reaching for my babies. I learned how to juggle one on each hip. "You should go."

"That's what I've been telling her," Brian added.

"I'm not into that," Logan defended. "I do my workouts here at home at my own pace."

"It's okay with me," Brian said. "I like the feel of extra softness late at night." Logan slapped Brian on the arm playfully.

"Why didn't you shower, Mo?" Logan asked. "You smell awful."

"Stop smelling me then."

"Well move downward so I can't."

"Ladies, ladies....not in front of the babies," Brian interrupted playfully.

"Well you know we have extra towels if you wanna freshen up before you get home," Logan suggested.

"Nah...I'll do it when I get home. Besides, Lance should be home now with Chantel and usually needs my help around this time of evening with her getting bathed. Though she can do it herself, she still needs assistance with the shower chair."

"Oh yeah, that's right," Brian said. His blue eyes and curly blonde hair shimmered in the sunset for some weird reason. Their kids were having so much fun they didn't even recognize I was there; which was good because Austin is very blunt about things and had the tendency of saying what was on his mind and I didn't need him telling me how I smelled. "Well, tell Lance I said hello and we gotta do the fishing trip soon."

"I will, Brian." Logan stood up to get the babies' belongings and helped me to my truck to load the babies and their bags. As I was pulling off, I turned on V103 to listen to some R&B. They were featuring Trey Songz' new CD and I had to admit...Can't Be Friends was not a song I needed to hear at that moment so I changed the dial to Magic 96.1. The S.O.S. Band was on point and made my fifteen minute ride home a breeze.

I pulled up into the driveway so thankful to be home. Lance was out in the front yard looking at the bricks of the walkway from the front door that leads to the sidewalk. After I put the truck in park and shut the engine off, Lance walked over and opened the rear passenger door and lifted Jayden out. I got Jayda out of the driver's side passenger door after grabbing my bag from the front seat. Lance walked around and greeted me with a kiss. "Mmm, you're nice and sweaty," he said.
"Thanks," I replied.
"How was class?"
"It was good."
"Good. Are you hungry?"
"No, not really. I just wanna get inside, shower off, and check on Chantel."
"Well, before you go inside, I want to tell you something."
"What?"
"I decided to let Tramarvious come over."
"Huh? Why?"
"Well...I've been keeping track of him."
"Lance! You have to stop doing that!"
"Yeah...right...anyway...he's been keeping himself outta trouble for some time now. Has a steady job...helping out his grandparents...I'm willing to let him prove to me what Chantel has been trying to sell me for months now."
I kissed my husband's cheek. "I'm proud of you, Sweetie."

"Yeah...well...thank me later," he said.

We entered the house and the smell of chicken teriyaki filled the air. Lamar and Keenan were home for the weekend and planned a dinner for their girlfriends, Alanna and Shakim, and Chantel and Tramarvious.

"Oh well...what is this?" I asked sampling some of the food on a serving platter.

"Chill, Mo-Ma!" Keenan said. "It's for our dates!"

"You're gonna starve me now?" I asked playfully.

"Dang...here...let me put you a plate to the side," Keenan declared. "Dad...can't y'all go somewhere tonight?"

"Hold on, now, are you paying the mortgage here?!" Lance asked with authority. "Don't think because you're all buffed up and got a new hottie you can bump your gums the wrong way. Now...you all have your fun in the den...Morgan and I will be off in our sanctuary with the babies."

"Eww, I know what that means," Keenan said. "Just give us the babies if y'all gonna be freakishly nasty."

"Boy, shut up!" Lamar said hitting Keenan on the shoulder.

"Naw, Lamar, they sound gross as hell. Old people just going at it like there's nobody else in the house sometimes." My mouth dropped, "You can *hear* us?"

"Sometimes," Keenan admitted smiling. "But I know where I get my skills from just from the sounds coming from behind that door."

"Boy that's enough!" Lance said embarrassed. He quickly went to the living room with Jayden in his arms. Keenan and Lamar continued to crack jokes as I shook my head walking away from them. The very thought of them hearing Lance and I made me feel a little uneasy too. I continued to my bedroom and put Jayda in the pack and play. Lance and Jayden came in also after I started to undress for a shower.

"I'm going to take Jayda in the shower with me so she could get used to the shower spray," I informed Lance.

"You know, I think that's a beautiful thing," Lance said. "It's on a whole level of bonding with the babies that I love to see you do."

"It's actually fun and I love how she reacts to the water and hold on to me making sure I don't let water get on her face. I still can't believe they're five months old now!"

Sighing, Lance replied, "Yeah...five months. Just think of this: you close your eyes one night and wake up the next realizing they're in college or on their way to college."

"I can't think of that now, I'm having too much fun watching them do baby things. I still can't believe I'm a mother at 32 years old."

"Mo, that's not old."

"I know, but practically every woman in my family had their kids before they reached 30. I mean some still had them over 30. Hmph...my great-grandmother had Grandmama when she was 44."

"Dang! She was still getting it, huh?"

I threw my sweaty work out shirt at Lance, "Hush!" After I was undressed, I undressed Jayda, grabbed our towels, and headed for the shower. As I stood in the shower holding my daughter, she reached for the water trying to catch it and at times tried to drink it from her hand. I lathered her up with her baby wash and just as I was about to rinse her off, she pooped in my arms.

"Oh, yuck!" I exclaimed. "LAAAAANNNNNCCCEEEEE!!!!"

Dashing in the bathroom, Lance questioned what was going on as he pulled the shower curtain back. He took one look at me and Jayda, noticed the baby poo, and started cracking up uncontrollably.

"You know...all you have to do is grab her so I can get situated in here," I declared.

With tears strolling down his face from laughter, Lance said, "I knew this was gonna happen one day! You should see your face!"

"Honey...get your daughter," I said calmly.

Doing as I requested, Lance took Jayda from me to finish cleaning her up and dressing her. I started washing myself off and laughed because only a baby could get away with taking a dump on their parent in the shower.

Two hours had passed and Lance and I were snuggled up in the bed playing with Jayda and Jayden. They were rolling over and trying to scoot across the bed. I looked at my kids and still couldn't believe that these two babies grew inside my body. They depended on my health, my blood, and my body as a whole just to make it here amongst the living. More and more they looked like their father though Jayda had my eyes and Jayden had my mouth. Jayden's skin was still light brown and Jayda wasn't as high yellow as I am like she was when she was born, but she was still light-skinned. I thought about earlier at my kickboxing class. I know people do tend to move on with their lives, and coincidences do happen, but something just didn't add up in my head with Victor. I hadn't seen this guy in ten years and all of a sudden he pops up in my town. Could Autumn have sold me out and told him my whereabouts? It just seemed too coincidental for her to pop up in town after writing to me and making a statement about Victor in her letter.

"Mo? Did you hear me?" Lance asked snapping me out of thought.

"I'm sorry, Sweetie, what did you say?"

"You okay?"

"Yeah, Lance, I'm good."

"You have that look on your face when you're in deep thought about something you don't need to be thinking of."

"And what look is that?"

"The look like you're ready to tear into someone."

"I was just thinking of Autumn."

"Yo! That was a trip! I mean...how do you marry someone you don't know? Mo...you should've heard Mark that night."

"What did he say?"

"He said he loved Autumn and still do. He got turned on to homosexuality in high school when one of his older friends came back to their hometown from Freak-Nic in Atlanta. Mark told Brian and I that he was attracted to girls and dated a few in high school, but was afraid to pursue sex from them. So Mark asked his friend, who he didn't know was bi, for some pointers one day he was at his house. Mark said his friend got undressed in front of him and pulled out a blow up doll he had in his closet. Mark said he watched his friend masturbate before he started giving him lessons on how to penetrate and gyrate but he became more intrigued by his friend doing himself. From that point on, he couldn't get that out of his head and whenever he tried to get with a girl, Mark's friend would pop up in his head. Mark didn't want to believe he was gay and denied it for years. But he said he'd have fantasies about guys more than girls and he knew it was wrong. Mo, the man had women *throwing* themselves at him that he knew were beautiful! He said he even allowed a few girls to blow him but while they did that he'd always imagine a guy or requested short haired girls who weren't very petite."

"So this is where Autumn comes in," I said. "She's not very small, but at one point she cut her hair short like Chantel's."

"Exactly. I tell you Mo, his story was a trip."

"It sounds like it. Actually, there's something else about Autumn that isn't adding up to me."

"Really? What?"

"I don't want to speculate yet, Lance. But I will. Once I do, I'll let you know."

## **Chapter Seven**

"So...let me get this straight: Victor Diez is now your kickboxing instructor?" Logan asked. I was at her house for our scheduled play date we have for the kids every Sunday after church.

"Yes," I answered.

"Morgan, you can't think this was a set up by Autumn. That girl honors the ground you walk on for saving her from Gerald back in college."

"Logan...c'mon! She sends me a letter telling me she's coming to town, mentions Victor in the same letter, then a few months later he pops up in Alpharetta, GA?"

"How do you know he hasn't been here before you? Or found a job here? You lived in Marietta for some time before you moved in with Lance. Remember Lance lived here first." Taking a sip of strawberry lemonade, I thought hard. Yes, Lance moved to Alpharetta a year after I moved to Marietta from Pittsburgh. So Victor could've been here long before Lance moved here. But my gut was telling me something different.

"Cookie," I began. "Something just ain't right."

"Okay, Mo. Suit yourself." Amira and Janelle, Logan's daughter and step-daughter, were playing with Jayden and Jayda showing them how to use ASL. I couldn't believe Amira was ten years old! She had excelled so much with her education after getting her cochlear implant and actually was able to talk now with her having speech therapy. Her speaking wasn't fully understood by those who didn't know her. But she was definitely able to speak and sign. Her thick, black hair was braided up into a ponytail and she looked so much like her late father, Amari. The same brown skin, eyes, nose, and smile. I still remember that awful day when her father tried to kill me and her mother and I still remember her mother pulling the trigger to save me.

"Amira," Logan said.

Amira looked up at her mother and answered, "Yes ma'am?"

"I love you."

"I love you too, Mom."

Smiling from ear to ear, Logan said to me, "Mo, you have no idea how much it means to me to hear my baby speak!"

"Yes, I do," I replied. "It sounds good to my ears also."

"So how has Janelle been lately?" Brian got full custody of Janelle years ago.

"She's been good. Not acting out a lot like before when Amira was able to get the cochlear and she couldn't." Janelle's level of hearing loss was so severe and profound that she was not a good candidate for the cochlear implant.

"So what are you gonna do, Mo? Are you gonna call Autumn again?"

"Yep. I just have to ask her."

"Well do it now and put it on speakerphone. I gotta hear this."

Doing what my sister suggested, I pulled my cell phone from my pocket of my painter's pants and began to dial. I hit the call button on the phone and listened to it ring four times before we heard her voice coming through the speaker.

"Hey, Autumn, what are you doing?" I asked.

"Sitting outside by the pool listening to music," Autumn responded. "You?"

"Sitting on the back porch at Logan's."

"Oh tell her hello for me!"

"Sure thing," I said smiling because she didn't know Logan was there. "So Autumn...tell me...and please, *please*, be honest with me. Did you tell Victor I was here?"

"What?! No! Why would I do that, Morgan?"

"It just all seemed coincidental that you'd write to me,

mention him in your letter, then he shows up in my town a month or so after you leave here."

"Listen, Morgan, you and your sister are the only women I consider true friends though we haven't seen each other for years. And knowing what Victor did to you, and lived to see it through, sickened me and still upsets me. Why would I sell you out like that?"

Logan hit me on the arm and mouthed *I told you* to me.

"Morgan, I know it all looked weird," Autumn began, "but you have to know in your heart that I wouldn't do anything like that to betray you. I put that on everything I love and have worked hard for."

"Okay...okay," I said. "I'll take your word. But I just don't get it."

"Ya know, there is this thing called social media. Maybe he was able to track you from there," Autumn announced.

"How? I didn't list where I currently live."

"Maybe not, but others could have put something on your timeline that said they were with you there."

Hmmm...I never thought of that. "You know, that's true. I gotta check out my timeline...see who said they were with me during the course of this year. But wouldn't we have mutual friends in order to see that?"

"Girl, for as smart as you are, you're kinda oblivious to this whole thing. Just check out your timeline and call me later. I'm doing my Sunday rituals before I start my work week."

"Will do. Take care, Autumn." I clicked off my phone and sat back in the light blue patio chair of Logan's.

"So, who do you think it was that put you out there?" Logan asked.

"I don't know. But I will find out. I just gotta really scroll through and check it out."

We were interrupted with our conversation when A.J. rolled up on the patio. His voice was changing and he was so hormonal he didn't know what to do with himself.

"Ma, I know it's a school night, but could I please go out with Mariana to the movies?"

"Huh?" Logan said. "Tonight?"

"Well, what about at 4? We're trying to see the other part of Transformers. C'mon, Ma, please?"

"And just why the urgency? Who's taking you? You know you can't go by yourselves."

"Ma! My other friends get to go without a chaperone. How come I can't?"

"Because I'm not your friends' mother. Now...who's going to take you?"

"I could ask Lamar, couldn't I Aunt Mo?"

"A.J. I don't know," I said. "Lamar and Keenan are heading back out to college around 5 o'clock."

"Man...we need more boys around here my age!" A.J. said storming off.

"Hey! Hey, hey, hey! Boy, bring your little brown behind back here!" Logan directed her son. A.J. slowly walked back to the patio and sat down across from his mother. Her lightly tanned skin had beads of sweat pouring out of her skin and her short coifed head tilted to the side sizing up her son. "Let me share something with you, you're 12...not 21. First of all, you're too damn young to consider yourself having a girlfriend, you've been in and outta trouble in school, and your grades have yet to get back to par. Now, I was going to take you until you just pulled that stunt. So call her up and tell her you can't go!"

"But...Ma...I'm sorry! Please! I promise I—"

"—I promise you I'll knock your nose off your face if you say one more word to me."

Silent for a while and biting his bottom lip, A.J. finally said, "Can I go to my room now?"

"Sure you can," Logan answered. "While you're at it, start

studying for your math quiz you have tomorrow and clean up that room."

"Yes, ma'am," A.J. said walking off carefully to his room. The one and only time he tried to have a tantrum with his mother by storming off and thinking he was going to yell back to her didn't go too well. Not only did she spank him, Brian got him, and so did Lance. He knows now to do as he's told and not to buck his mother. Shaking my head I said, "I'm not ready for that!"

"Mo, enjoy your bopsie twins now. The older they get, the more I struggle to keep my patience. But I wouldn't trade being a mother for anything in the world. Now...back to this Victor-ordeal."

"I'm gonna do it later on when I get home."

"Why? I'll just get my laptop and when can do it now." Walking with Jayden on her hip into her house, Logan swiftly walked in to get her laptop. The whole time I kept thinking about where I've been recently and who I've been with. The only thing that comes to mind is Lance's family reunion back in July. There were a lot of people there and I did take some pictures with his sisters, mom, dad, and other relatives I've gotten to know in the past few years. Logan came back out with her laptop tucked under her right arm and my son on her left hip. With Jayda on my lap, I took the laptop from her before it slipped out of her grip. After setting the laptop on the patio table, I opened it and started the boot up process. It took all of three minutes to boot up the computer and log on to the social media site. After I got logged on, I went to my timeline and started researching. I went back to The Brooks' family reunion where I was tagged in a few pictures and I started scrolling through it thoroughly. I noticed five pictures which had a lot of likes from friends of friends. One picture was of Lance and I with our kids, the other was with Miss Rochelle and I with her daughters, another was with just Teri, Finesse, and myself...but nothing too obvious where I could see how Victor would know my whereabouts.

"Did you find anything?" Logan asked.

"Nope," I responded. "Nothing. But I'll be doing this for hours. It's going to take a lot more than a tagged picture."

"Well, Mo, it just might be coincidental. That happens a lot."

"Girl, you're too optimistic for me sometimes. I have to go against you on this one."

"Suit yourself. So how's Chantel coming along?"

"Oh, she's doing great! She's dedicated to her therapy and using her walker to the fullest. I remember when it was believed that she was going to be paralyzed forever. God is good."

"Amen to that!"

"Cookie, I look at her every single day and just get inspired by her strength to continue to progress. But I know a lot of it is Tramarvious. I can admit...we were so wrong about him. That young man was devoted to changing his ways and he's sticking to that vow. But for him to be so young and dedicated to Chantel...makes me believe young love is real and it wasn't a figment of my imagination when we were that age."

"Well, for as hard as you were...and still is...you were always the softee when it came to matters of the heart."

"Whatever." I logged off of Logan's laptop and stood up with Jayda in my arms. "Cookie, it's time for me to roll out. Gotta get situated for the evening. You know...my pre-work day rituals."

"Yeah, I understand. The kids gotta get ready for school tomorrow anyway. Let me help you with the babies."

As Logan and I were gathering the babies' bags and getting them locked into their car seats, her children all came around, except A.J., to give us kisses and hugs. This is what it was all about for me. My family and the love I have for my sister and her kids.

"Ma! Mama!" screamed A.J. running out of the house with the telephone in his hand.

"What boy?! What's the matter?!" Logan yelled back.

"It's Ma Belle on the phone. She said Grandmama just passed!"

Logan and I stood motionless like statues next to my truck. I felt my heart sink and my knees buckle. I held on to the driver's door of the truck to keep from falling on the concrete. Logan took the phone from A.J. and started talking to our mother. I was still trying to put that sentence together in my head. My grandmother is dead? The woman who raised me when my mother couldn't? I heard Logan's voice talking on the phone but I was incoherent. I should've gone up there like Lance wanted. I should've gone up there when Logan first said something was going on. I should've gone up there when Grandmama asked me to. Logan's relationship with Grandmama was different than mine. When I was 10, Logan and I had to live with her because our mother was unstable. However, when we were about to start high school, Logan moved with our aunt in Homewood so she could go to the high school for that jurisdiction. All of the laughter, the tears, and words of wisdom...gone. I could never hear her voice in person, smell her favorite soap she used on her skin, and most of all, get one of those awesome and loving hugs.

"Mo...Mo...Morgan!" Logan said shaking me until I acknowledged her.

"How? What happened?" I whispered as I was still leaning on my truck.

"Mo, she had a stroke. She was found in her chair unresponsive by Aunt Ivory who showed up to take her to the doctor's. It's a good thing Aunt Ivory had a key. No telling how long it would've been before anyone else went over there." Putting her hands on my shoulders and pulling me in to hug me, Logan whispered, "Mo, I know how much you loved and adored her. I did too. But we gotta go home and pay our final respects."

Home. The family. Everything I worked to get away from was coming at me full circle.

"I don't think you should drive home, Mo."

"I'll be fine," I breathlessly replied.

"Are you sure?"

"Yes. I'll call you when we get in the door." Hugging each other goodnight, I told Logan how much I loved her and she did the same with me. I climbed in my truck and proceeded to go home. The whole ride home, I thought of my grandmother. How she taught me how to cook, how to sew a button on a shirt, and lectured me on not being feminine and worried about me being too much of a tomboy. She loved the fact that I married someone who was not Kevin and enjoyed seeing me walk down the aisle to get married. Now, I had to live on with her memory and accept she isn't here anymore amongst the living.

When I arrived home, I saw Lance's Trail Blazer in the driveway. I tooted the horn three times to let him know I was outside of the house so he could help me with the twins. Within the next minute, he came outside drenched in sweat and his workout gear. If my heart wasn't hurting at that moment, I'd try to tackle him because he was looking more handsome than I could remember. I stepped out of the vehicle and allowed him to kiss my forehead before he got Jayda out of the car. As he was doing so, he asked, "How was your Sunday play date?"

I couldn't say a word. I had a lump in my throat and I felt my eyes burn with tears I tried to hold back. Lance looked

at me and before he started to get Jayda, he grabbed my arms and looked me into my eyes with deep concern.
"Mo...what—"
"She's dead!" I cried. "Grandmama's dead! My Grandmama left me!" I felt myself being wrapped up in my husband's arms as he tried to hold me tightly against his body. "It hurts, Lance! It hurts! She's gone! I should've gone home when she asked me to!"
I guess all of my crying and screaming got the attention of Alanna and Chantel because they eventually came outside. I cried and screamed uncontrollably not caring who heard me or saw me. The only other time I lost my composure like this is when Kevin Littleton cheated on me and I retaliated. But this was a whole different level of hurt and I didn't cry and pour out my heart like this. Kevin was a first love. My grandmother was my world next to Lance, our children, and Logan's family.
"Alanna, come and get the babies," Lance instructed. Alanna walked over and got Jayda out of the car first. She then walked over and balanced her baby brother in her other arm once she got him out of the car and carried them both in the house. Chantel was standing with her walker next to the kitchen door entrance to the house. She eventually went inside. Lance's sweaty body contained me and comforted me as I stood in our driveway mourning my grandmother. In a few days, off to Pittsburgh we had to go.

I tried to sleep that night but it was hard. I just kept replaying over and over in my head how Logan and Lance told me how much Grandmama wanted to see us and I just kept putting it off. When I finally went to sleep, I traveled to another suppressed memory of my childhood.
********************************************************

December 1987. Logan and I were gawking over our new little brother, James. He was born on the 2$^{nd}$ and had just come home. Our mother was in the bathroom and her boyfriend was in their bedroom getting high with some of his drug buddies. Logan and I had to make room for his crib in our room which already had two twin beds and one large dresser for us to share. Imagine a crib in the midst of all of that.

"Isn't he cute?" Logan said as we stood over his crib watching him sleep.

"Yeah," I agreed.

"I wonder what he's going to look like when he grows up."

"Well, he won't be light-skinned like us," I said.

"He could be," Logan replied. "He's kinda light now."

"Nah. His daddy is brown like Ma. No way that's gonna happen. Besides...Grandmama said Black babies change colors."

"We didn't change, Mo."

"It's because we took after our daddy."

"Hmph. I wish I was brown-skinned. I hate being light-skinned! I'm tired of everybody trying to pick on us and calling us names all of the time! And I'm tired of you fighting all of the time about it."

"Well, as long as girls pick on us, I'm gonna knock 'em out like I always do! You need to start fighting back, Logan, and stop being scared."

"I don't know how to fight, Mo."

"I'll teach you. Let's go in the living room so we don't wake the baby."

Logan and I walked out of our bedroom and into the living room. We pushed the table against the wall so we could have an open floor.

"Now...put your dukes up like this," I instructed Logan as I stood in my best boxing stance. "When you see my fist come at you, block it. Don't let me hit you." I threw my fist at Logan's face and she ducked back.

"Good move! Now no matter what, defend yourself."

I threw another punch toward her face and she shoved it out of the way. However, she wasn't ready for me to push her then tackle her to the floor.

"Why did you do that?" she cried.

"Get up, Cookie," I said helping her up. "I said, no matter what, defend yourself." I got back in my boxing stance and starting throwing air punches. One of them landed in her right eye and I didn't stop until she fought me back. We pushed, punched, and pulled each other around the whole living room. I ended up sitting on Logan's chest and she tried to knock me off her. I playfully slapped her in the face as if I was going to punch her until I felt a heavy closed hand punch connect to my head with so much force it knocked me off of her.

"You think you can just beat up on your sister?!" my mother yelled. She grabbed my hair on the back of my head to make me stand up.

"Mama, I wasn't—"

"Shut up! I saw what you were doing!" My mother pushed me against the wall and punched me in my stomach until all the air was knocked out of me and I collapsed to the floor.

"Mama! Please..."Logan begged.

"Get up and fight me, Morgan, since you think you're so big and bad!" My mother yelled. I stayed curled up on the floor. As much as I was hurt, I became enraged. But I knew she'd kill me if I tried or even thought about hitting her.

"Oh...you don't wanna cry?! Oh you mad?!" I looked up and noticed she was snatching a belt off of her waist. With the strap in her hand, she hit me with the buckle repeatedly in my back and one time, it even hit my mouth. Logan sat on the couch in terror and cried. Eventually, Daniel, my mom's boyfriend, surfaced into the living room.

"Belle! Stop!" he demanded taking the belt from her. I did nothing but lie on the floor in the fetal position. "What the fuck's wrong with you?! She's a child! *Your* child! Do you have any idea what would happen to you if their father finds the shit out?!"

"He don't want them!" my mother said. "If he did, he'd come get them some time! But he's out having other kids with other females. Besides...they have you now, Daniel."

"Belle," Daniel began. He was so jacked up on dope his eyes were bloodshot. "You know you wrong for this. Leave her alone." Daniel reached down to pick me up. As much as I want to pull away from him since he molested me the night before, he made me feel protected. Weird, huh? When I got to my feet I walked over and sat next to Logan. She sat there stiff as a board with fright and tears streaming down her face. My bottom lip was cracked from getting hit in the mouth with the belt buckle. I felt the left side of my face pulsate from the blow I took to the face from my mother. I knew I was going to have bruised face as I did before whenever she'd hit me.

"I'm tired of Morgan bullying Logan!" my mom yelled.

"I wasn't bullying—" I started to say until she marched over and slapped me in the mouth.

"Now you're back-talking me?! I saw you!"

"We were playing," I cried. "I wasn't hurting her."

"Oh...now you cry. Good! Take your ass outside for a while; both of you!"

"Belle, it's kind of cold out," Daniel said.

"I want them outta here! They can bundle up; shit they're kids!"

I jumped up off of the couch and ran to get my coat, scarf, boots, and hat. Logan was right behind me. After we put on our winter gear, we dashed out the door.

We were outside in the court of the apartment building we lived in. I hated living in the projects. The chilled late fall air hit me in the face and numbed my face where my mother punched me.

"Mo, I'm sorry," Logan said. Her cheeks had dried tear marks on them and they stood out in the cold air.

"For what?" I asked.

"Getting you in trouble."

"You didn't. C'mon. Let's get some dinner at Grandmama's." Logan and I walked to the other side of Bonifay Street in Saint Clair Village until we got to our grandmother's building. We called it the senior building because every tenant in her building was over 45 years old with the exception of two families. It was the cleanest and quietest apartment building in the whole community. When we got there, I knocked on Grandmama's door. At the time, she was 48 years old and was able to maneuver pretty quickly. She was still sporting a Jheri Curl and had streaks of gray appearing in her hair. When she opened the door, the smell of fried chicken hit my nostrils.

"What y'all doin' here?" Grandmama asked. Though she lived in Pittsburgh since the age of 15, she still had that southern drawl. She moved to the side so we could walk in. I started taking off my winter gear as I walked to the back room to put my coat and other belongings in what we called the coat chair. Logan was right behind me. I darted into the bathroom to look into the mirror. My lip was swollen and cut and my face was bruised. I looked into the medicine cabinet for some colored lip gloss Grandmama sometimes kept for Logan to play with. I found the pink sparkly lip gloss and put on so much of it that the cut was covered. I started looking for Aunt Ivory's foundation. Though she was a cinnamon brown woman, I used what I could to try and cover my face. Being that I was 10 years old, I thought I was doing good.

"Mo! C'mon in here! Your food's on the table!" Grandmama yelled down the hall.

I washed my hands and cleaned up as much as I could of the makeup in the sink and proceeded to the kitchen table. Mmmm....homemade mashed potatoes, corn on the cob, and fried chicken. This beat pork 'n beans and hot dogs anyday!

"Hey now," Grandmama said looking at me. "You been fighting again?"

Keeping my focus on my plate, I lied and said, "Yes ma'am."

"Chile, you ain't no boy! Stop rough-housin' out there," she said.

"She's lying, Grandmama," Logan confessed.

"Logan!" I grunted.

"Ma's been beating her up again," Logan continued. "Every time you see her face like this or marks on her body is because of Ma."

"What?!" Grandmama asked. She stopped eating, stood up and walked over to me. "Morgan Taylor Hixon-Chambers...is this true?"

"And Daniel's been touching her too. I see it every night when he comes in our room and thinks I'm asleep," Logan added.

"Logan! Shut up!" I yelled.

"Morgan! Is all of what she's saying true?" Grandmama asked with panic in her eyes.

I nodded my head up and down.

"W—why didn't you say somethin'? Answer me!" Grandmama demanded.

"Because I'm scared she's gonna hurt me if I tell," I said.

Standing back in disbelief, Grandmama looked as if she was about to blow.

"Y'all stay here and eat your food. Don't worry...y'all ain't going back home."

"But what about James?" Logan asked me in a whisper. "Logan, shut up and eat," I said. I felt so betrayed by my sister. She ratted me out and made me look worse than I felt.

About three hours passed when my mother knocked on Grandmama's door. It started to get dark early and since we weren't home when the street lights came on, she knew where we were because we've done it before plenty of times. With James bundled up in her arms, my mother walked in after Grandmama opened the door. Logan and I were in the back bedroom watching a movie on the VCR she had just for us. All of a sudden we hear Grandmama beckon, "Logan...Morgan...get in here!"
We walked down the hall and into the living room side by side. Our mother was sitting in the rocking chair with James. Grandmama sat on the love seat across from her.
"Belle, now you tell me what happened to this gal?"
"I—I don't know. Morgan, what—"
"Stop right there! You gonna start lyin' before you think about what you're sayin' to me?"
"Ma, I—"
"—You what, Belle? You been beatin' on this gal all this time and tellin' me she out here fightin' and carryin' and it's really been *you*? And you lettin' that...that...crackhead feel on her?"
"I haven't been—"
"Logan told me everything, Belle! *Everything!* Now I don't know how you think you gonna sit here and try to bullshit me, but let it be known that from this day on, these girls are staying with me! Now, you tell that crackhead to pack up all of their stuff and bring it over here tonight! I don't understand you! I've never put my hands on you like that! You and your sister and brothers had all the love you could

ever want from your daddy and me and you do this to these girls! I didn't raise you like this, Belle! Now...I could take that baby, but I ain't got it in me to take care of a newborn. So get your ass outta here and bring the girls' things back here *tonight!*"

"Fine, Momma! Keep 'em! You're doing me a big justice anyway! I'm sick of looking at them and seeing their father every damn day!"

"Get yo ignorant tail outta here! Ya ain't gotta worry about that no mo'!"

Without further word, my mother left with James. I started to think it was a bad idea to for him to be there and I felt bad.

"Logan, we need to try to get Grandmama to keep James," I said.

"How?" she asked.

"I don't know. But we gotta think of something."

"Mo, didn't you hear what Ma said? She don't want us because we look like our father. She's not gonna hurt James because he's brown-skinned."

"I heard. But what if James' skin color don't change?"

"Let's pray it does so he doesn't get hurt too. After all, she already sent Joseph away. I hope she doesn't get rid of him too."

After eavesdropping and discussing our theories on genetics, Logan and I went back to watching *Howard the Duck* and for the first time in a long time, I felt safe. I didn't worry about who was coming into my room at night to touch me or grope me and I didn't have to worry about being hit. I didn't have to hear my mother and Daniel have sex in the next room or come home from school and find them in the living room getting high. I was finally going to have some normalcy with my sister.

\*\*\*\*\*\*\*\*\*\*\*\*\*\*\*\*\*\*\*\*\*\*\*\*\*\*\*\*\*\*\*\*\*\*\*\*\*\*\*\*\*\*\*\*\*\*\*\*

December 9, 2009. Logan's family and my family arrived in Pittsburgh to get ready for Grandmama's funeral. Because there's so many of us, we ended up renting an entire bed and breakfast for three days. Chantel, Alanna, Lamar, and Keenan took the downstairs because it was easier for Chantel to maneuver and they wanted to assist her as much as possible. Logan, Brian, and their kids took the second floor, and Lance and I with the twins on the third floor. After living somewhere for more than eight years on one floor, these stairs just to get to our room was a workout in itself. We arrived in Pittsburgh at 6pm. In Shadyside on Fifth Avenue, we stayed at The Cozy Bed and Breakfast; an old Victorian style home that used to belong to an elite family back in the early 1900s. It was furnished with elegant plush living room furniture, 16x20 wall pictures of forestry, fresh flower arrangements, and a big, elegant, Chandelier. All three bathrooms were renovated with up-to-date bathroom fixtures, and the kitchen was something out of a catalog. White marble countertops, an electric eye-less stovetop, and a huge refrigerator stocked with complementary bottled water, fruit, and other beverages. The floors were made of bubinga and the walls were painted in a neutral earth tone that wasn't familiar to me but was absolutely beautiful. All of the bedrooms were either earth tone or ocean inspired and had lightly scented lavender air freshener plugged into an outlet. Lance, Brian, Lamar, Keenan, and A.J. carried the luggage to our rooms. Amira, Aleasha, Janelle, and Austin went to their rooms to investigate and decide who was going to sleep in which bed. Logan and I went to talk to the house owner Miss Celeste Green. She was a short, slim woman with black hair and gray streaks. Her dark brown eyes stood out on her somewhat pale skin. She had been in the office/den getting the paperwork together with our invoice, information, keys, and rules.

"Hello, Ladies!" Miss Green said with a warm smile. "I'm so glad you all made it safely."

"Thank you for having us," Logan said extending her hand out to shake Miss Green's hand.

"My pleasure," Miss Green replied. "I hope that I'm able to accommodate your family to the best of my ability. This home has been in my family for over a hundred years. Though my mother wasn't happy when my brother and I decided to make this into a bed and breakfast, she couldn't argue too much when she started to see the revenue we were getting. With that, my brother and I vowed to make our family home a home for others who needed a home to sleep in; not some plushy or rundown hotel. Now...here are your invoices, rules, contact numbers, and keys. The chef will be here in the morning to make breakfast and to see if you'll need him for lunch and dinner. If so, that'll be an extra fee. Otherwise, you can feel free to cook your own meals. However, if you cook, please wash the dishes. The cleaning crew normally comes in around 1pm to check the trash, bathrooms, and kitchen. If you request, we can have clean sheets and towels everyday as well. If there's an emergency, please refer to your booklet, and your payment will be expected the day you leave. Any questions?"

"Umm, I think we have everything," I answered. "Thank you, Miss Green."

"You're more than welcome," Miss Green said.

Logan and I walked to the living room and sat down with the twins.

"Mo, this couch is *comfortable!* I have to get this set!" Logan announced.

"Yeah, it is!" I agreed. "This is something I can see in our living room. Just convincing Lance to get it is the obstacle."

"Well, all I have to do is give Brian some extra vitamin P

with a twist of stripper and throat and I can get anything I ask for."

"Eww...TMI...TMI!"

"Mo, I don't even know why you're acting like a nun. You're the one that gave me instructions on how to make my man happy behind closed doors."

"Yeah, but...eww!"

"Mama," A.J. said walking into the living room, "we have everything in the rooms. Can I hook up the Xbox?"

"Umm, I don't know, A.J. Mo, are we going to Grandmama's tonight or tomorrow?"

I shrugged my shoulders. "I honestly don't know. Wait...I thought we were going there tomorrow afternoon?"

"I guess you can, Son," Logan said. "Make sure you check in on the girls and Austin."

"Oh, Austin and Aleasha are watching cartoons. Amira and Janelle are doing their nails and all that other girly stuff."

"Okay," Logan said.

"Ma, promise me we'll never move here. It's too cold," A.J. said.

"Honey," Logan began, "I have no desire in ever moving back here for that very reason."

Smiling, A.J. said, "Thank you! I'll be playing my game now."

"Logan," Brian said walking into the living room to Logan, "what do you want for dinner? We're getting hungry and I don't know too much about the eateries up here."

"Well, you're not going to find any soul food places, Bojangles, Captain D's, or Sonny's Bar-B-Q."

"Are you kidding me?" Brian signed in ASL.

"I'm serious," Logan signed back.

Vocally, Brian said, "Well what do you have up here?"

"A bunch of Italian, Polish, Jewish, and Asian food restaurants besides major national food chains."

"Wait, wait," Keenan said coming from the room he and Lamar are sharing, "there's no Bojangles up here?"

"Nope," I answered.

"No Captain D's?" Lamar asked right behind him.

"Unh-unh," Logan stated.

"What da hell, man?" Keenan said. "This is gonna be a problem. I gotta have Bojangles' Bo-Berry biscuits in the morning!"

"Well, Keenan...not this time," I said.

At this point, everyone started to come into the living room except for Logan and Brian's kids who were having fun playing upstairs from the sounds of things. Chantel and Alanna came into the living room and sat down on two high-back chairs. Keenan and Lamar stood at the fireplace and Brian and Lance sat next to me and Logan.

"Well, we gotta do something about some food," Lance remarked. "I'm pretty sure the kids are starving too."

"Hmm," Logan began, "how about we go to The Golden Corral?"

"Oh, no!" I exclaimed. "No way. We do better getting some pizza and hoagies from Pizza Milanos."

"I'm down," Lamar said.

"Me too," Chantel chimed.

"Alright; it's settled," Lance declared. "Mo...Logan...since y'all know more about this place, how about you two go and grab us something? Brian and I can stay with the kids."

"I'm going too," Keenan said.

"Me also," Lamar replied.

"Well, y'all can be out in Antarctica," Alanna said. "I'm staying here where there's some heat. I gotta call Shakim anyway."

Without further ado, Logan, Lamar, Keenan, and I ventured off to the pizza shop to get some food.

We piled up in Lance's new Suburban that he bought a few months back just for road trips. It still had the new car smell and was so clean on the inside that he didn't allow anyone to eat or drink in it. The brisk beginning of winter air hit our faces and brought back many memories of my childhood and teenage years.

"Mo-Ma," Keenan started, "what's the women like up here?"

"I knew it, I knew it, I knew it!" Lamar said. "You can't go anywhere without trying to scoop up a lady."

"It's the heterosexual American way! I'm young, handsome, single, and having fun."

Logan turned around in the passenger's seat and asked, "Keenan, what happened to your girlfriend? Uh...Tiona?"

"She dumped him for another girl!" Lamar announced laughing.

"Shut up, man! That wasn't it!" Keenan said defensively. "Okay..maybe a little, Aunt Logan."

"Please explain!" Logan said teasingly.

Keenan sat back cool as he tried to be and started telling his story. "See...what happened was she suggested trying to add some flavor to our relationship by asking one of her girls to join in one night. I said cool! I'm figuring...I'm living the dream! Then, it started to become her request, like, every other time we went at it. One day she just came out and said she's feeling more appreciated and loved by her girl and said the only time I wanted to see her was when I wanted some tail."

"Well wasn't it though?" Lamar asked. "Because the only time you did anything with her was to get in her drawers."

"Naw, man! Aye...look...I was feeling Tiona but I think it had a lot to do with the fact that her girl was able to take my—"

"Hey, hey, hey!" I said. "Keenan, honey, I love you but I really don't wanna hear about your bedroom antics or your anatomy or anything connected to anything personal about your sex life anymore."

"Alright, Mo-Ma. My bad. Long story short, she chose to be with a chick."

Lamar added, "And she knew Keenan was seeing other ladies."

"Keenan!" Logan said. "Is that true?"

"Well...yeah. I mean, I'm a pimp, Aunt Lo. I have many thoroughbreds in my stable."

"I don't understand how you're the polar opposite of your father when you've been with him solely for over ten years," Logan replied.

"No offense to you Mo-Ma, but I've seen how my dad was with my mom. It was obvious he wasn't happy and he stayed with her because of us. Then we moved to Georgia. Dad had mad game before y'all hooked up, Mo-Ma! I mean...he had dimes trying to get at him all the time!"

"Uh, Bro? Do you think you ought to be telling her this?" Lamar tried to calmly and quietly ask Keenan.

"Man, Mo-Ma got him now. It shouldn't matter what happened before that."

I exhaled sharply. Little did my step-sons know, I am a very jealous woman and he was putting a lot of little thoughts in my head about my husband.

"Yo, man...it's about respect. Chill, Keenan," Lamar said.

"Yeah," I added. "I think you should listen to your brother, Keenan."

We pulled up to the pizza shop and entered after I parked. We all went inside and placed a very large order. After about 20 minutes, we were back in the Suburban on the way to the bed and breakfast. After we served the pizza, hoagies, and drinks, we all got the little ones settled for the night. Alanna and Chantel were on their phones talking to their boyfriends. Keenan and Lamar were playing Xbox with

A.J. until a knock rapped on the front door.

"Are you expecting anyone?" Lance asked.

"No," Logan and I answered simultaneously and in confusion.

Lance cautiously went to the front door and opened it. On the outside was a tall, young man with deep dimples and smooth brown sugar skin.

"Can I help you?" Lance asked.

"Yes, I'm looking for Logan and Morgan," the young man said. "I was told they'd be here."

"Hold on a sec," Lance instructed and closed the door. He never let anyone into the house he didn't know at home without conferring with me first.

"Mo, there's some guy out here asking for you and Logan. Somehow he knew y'all would be here?"

Logan jumped up and exclaimed, "James! James is here!"

"No...way!" I yelled. We both ran to the front door almost knocking Lance out of the way. Logan opened the door and squealed. James had the biggest smile on his face when he looked at us. We didn't give him a chance to walk in because we surrounded him and hugged him and kissed him.

"Come in! Come in! It's cold out here!" Logan ordered.

Closing the door behind us, we walked in and introduced our brother to our husbands and children. Eagerly and excitedly, Logan did all of the talking as she did when she was happy.

"Brian, Lance, this is our little brother, James! James, this is my husband Brian and Mo's husband Lance!"

Brian and Lance stood up and greeted our brother with a handshake.

"Nice to finally meet you," Brian said.

"Same here," Lance said. "We've heard about you for some time."

"I've heard about y'all too," James said. Standing at 6'4", he towered over all of us.

"Sorry we had to meet on these terms," Lance said.

"Yeah," James replied. "It's cool. I've been meaning to make my way down there but with my job and all, it's been hard for me to make time for myself."

"Well, it's never too late to make the plan happen," Lance replied. "I'm gonna get all of the kids so you can meet them."

"Thank you," I said to Lance. "So, little-big brother, what's been going on?"

James followed us into the living room and sat in one of the high back chairs Lance sat in. He took off his black Kangol and unwrapped the scarf from around his neck leaving his black pea coat on. "Nothing at all. You know...working, finishing up school, paying bills."

"When are you gonna leave this dump and do something different?" Logan asked sitting on his lap like a big kid sitting on Santa. By this time, I was holding both of my babies.

"Oh it's in the plans," James said. "But I don't know if I wanna go. I mean, I've traveled to a lot of spots and was impressed, but I don't know."

"Let me guess," I began, "you don't wanna leave your mother, right?"

"Partly," James admitted. "But I mean I'm working for Port Authority bringing in $40,000 a year."

"For real?" Logan questioned.

"Yeah," James responded. "I mean I'm bringing in some cash. That's a lot to give up."

"You remember our cousin Courtney worked for Port Authority," I said. "He and Shelby moved to Florida after he was able to get on with their transit system there. Maybe you ought to look into that option."

James' eyes lit up. "Yeah! Florida! I've been down there...they have plenty of boulders!"

"Boulders?" Logan asked. "What are you talking about?"

"He's talking about females with big asses," Keenan said walking into the living room. Logan stood up and introduced them to one another.

"Yo, man...how old are you?" Keenan asked James.

"I'm 22," James replied.

"Yeah! That's what I'm talking about! Somebody from around this way who can take me around that's close to my age! Whatchu be getting' into up here, man?"

"Man, I be working and going to school. I'm tryna save up some cash so I can buy a house."

"Yo, man...you my step-mother's brother and all....you ain't gonna have me calling you uncle or none of that?"

Laughing heartedly, James said, "No! That's crazy and weird as hell! Naw, man, we cool!"

"That's what's up!" Keenan said. Turning to his left, he introduced James to Lamar, Alanna, and Chantel. Logan's brood came downstairs and they all met their uncle and were so mesmerized by his stature.

Around 10:30 that night, all of the younger kids were sleeping. Chantel and Alanna watched movies. James took Keenan and Lamar to the Strip District. Brian and Logan were in their room; Lance and I were in our room with the babies. Once they were asleep and we all showered, Lance and I lied down and spooned. Rubbing my left arm since it was facing the ceiling, Lance kissed my neck and said, "I love you, Morgan."

"I love you too, Lance."

"How are you feeling?"

Exhaling I said, "Sleepy. Tired. Exhausted."

"No, no, no. I mean how you are emotionally?"

"I'm holding on. Still trying to accept Grandmama isn't here."

"Mmm. I understand. You know...your brother seems really grounded to be so young."

"Yeah, he does. I'm so happy that he's making it."

"What about your other brother...uh...Joseph?"

"I haven't heard from him since he went to juvie."

"Where's he at now?"

"I don't know. If he shows up at the funeral it'll be the first time I've seen him or talked to him in over ten years."

"He's younger or older than James?"

"Older. However, Joseph was sent away when he was five years old to military school under his father's direction. Why that happened is still unclear to this day. James went to live with him when he and my mother broke up when James was about ten years old."

"Wow."

"I don't understand it though. I mean, Daniel was strung out on dope bad."

"Maybe he got cleaned up before he took him."

"Possibly." After a couple of moments of silence, I said, "I'm not ready for this. I'm not ready to see my grandmother in a casket."

"You're not alone, Honey. I'm here with you."

"Lance, promise me that whatever happens you don't allow me to lose myself. The situation with my mother is a volatile one. Trust me."

"I got you, Mo. I got you."

*************************************************

The next morning, we all rose to the smell of bacon and sausage cooking at 6:30am. The chef was there just as Miss Green said he would be. It was a good thing he did come early because we probably would've slept too late and being that there were six children there to get ready, Logan and I needed the extra time even though our husbands were with us. The first person in the kitchen was Alanna. Covered in her long, yellow housecoat she went in to eat first. Or at least she tried. The chef, David, didn't allow one person to eat if they were a family unit. He felt everyone should be present to break bread together.

"Sir," Alanna started, "you don't understand. My brothers and little cousin are greedy. If I don't get a plate now, I'll starve."

While scrambling eggs and flipping a pancake, David turned to Alanna and said, "Ma'am, what you do when you're home is different than what I do when I serve families."

"You don't have to call me ma'am. I recently turned 17 last month," Alanna snapped.

"You don't have to call me sir. I'm only 27," David quipped back. His straight white teeth lined his perfectly sculptured face on his olive skin. Alanna knew he was of a mixed race, but didn't want to pry.

"Well what do I call you?" Alanna asked. At this point she was flirting.

"David," he answered.

"I'm Alanna. Nice to meet you."

"Yeah, I'll say," Lance said walking in the kitchen. "You're doing the thing in here! Smells like Ihop."

"I do my best," David replied smiling.

"Alanna, are you trying to get your food first again?"

"Yes, Sir. But David wouldn't let me."

Cocking his head to the side, Lance starting looking at his daughter and wondering why the two were on a first name basis. Alanna was twirling the end of her hair and she usually done when a guy was around that she was attracted to.

"David, right?"

David nodded yes while finishing home fries.

"How much longer before everything is done?" Lance asked.

"Oh, about another five minutes," he answered.

"Okay. Alanna, go get the family and have a seat in the dining area."

Disappointed, Alanna did as she was told. Lance sat on one of the kitchen stools and just watched David for a while.

"So, uh...David, right?" Lance began.

"Yes, that's right," David answered.

"Is this your main gig? You know...cooking in a bed and breakfast?" Lance asked.

While dumping the home fries in a serving bowl for our families, David laughed, "No, it isn't. I do this every now and then to help out Miss Green when I'm in town. I actually own a couple of bistros in Richmond, VA."

"Is that right?" Lance asked a little impressed.

"Yep. I earned my dues as a culinary artist. I love to cook."

"I bet you do well with the ladies having that trade," Lance insinuated.

"Mr. Brooks, right?" David asked.

"Call me Lance."

"Okay then, Lance. Listen, my private life is my private life. But you don't have to worry about your daughter. Though she's beautiful, she's too young and my fiancee' is my world."

Smiling with a sigh of relief, Lance said, "My man! You need help with anything?"

"Nope. I got it."

I had just got done with feeding, cleaning, and clothing the twins when Logan came up to my room.

"Hey, Mo, you need any help?"

"Nah. I'm good."

"Mo...are you okay? You look drained."

"Cookie, I don't think I can do this." Tears started streaming down my face.

Hugging me, Logan said, "Mo, it's okay. Death is a part of life. It's bound to happen. But you know as well as I know Grandmama loved you exponentially."
Sniffling I said, "I know."
"Look into yourself, into your heart, and into your spirit for strength. None of us were expecting this, but you're not alone."
I hugged my sister and for the first time, she actually consoled me. I've never been this emotional or have cried this long. Even after our grandfather passed away 20 years prior.
"C'mon, Mo, let's go eat so we can get to the church. I'll take Jayden. My kids are already downstairs."
Following my sister downstairs, I felt anxious. I didn't want to bury my grandmother and I was emotionally a wreck. However, I had to put on a positive attitude for my kids.

When we got downstairs to the dining room, we sat at a very long and extravagant spread. There were 13 of us who sat at the table. Lance and Brian sat at the head of the table on each end, Logan and I sat next to our husbands, and our children sat on the same side we sat. The babies were in high chairs close to Lance and I. Though they already ate upstairs, we gave them some soft fruit to eat. Lance blessed the food and everyone began to dig in. David did us well! Bacon, sausage, scrambled eggs, home fries, pancakes, biscuits, and fruit salad. Coffee, milk, orange and apple juice was on the buffet at the back of the dining room. While we ate, the typical behaviors surfaced. A.J. wanting to distance himself away from his siblings and toward Keenan and Lamar; Brian, Amira, and Janelle discussing ASL etiquette; Alanna and Chantel were talking about going back to Georgia; Keenan and Lamar talking about their night with James.

At 10:30am, we arrived at Missionary Baptist Church on Webster Avenue. There were already droves of cars lined up and down the street and we had to park almost a block away from the church. I felt my stomach bubble and my heart race as I approached the many relatives there to say their final goodbyes to my grandmother. Many cousins that Logan and I played with as kids and their parents were there as well as two great-aunts from out of town and other out of town family. Logan's family and my family exited out cars and walked as an army toward the church. Lance held Jayda and I held Jayden. Then, I see not only my brother James, but my other brother Joseph. My beige brother Joseph walked up to me with a smile and gave me the biggest hug I've ever gotten from him.

"Sup, Sis," his very deep voice said in my ear. He smelled as if he just smoked a cigarette and took a drink of liquor. When we parted, I took a look at him since I hadn't seen him in over 10 years. His beard was closely shaven to his face and it looked as if he aged from the streets and from time in jail. Joseph looked like life had gotten the best of him; he looked hard, sullen, and emotionless.

"How are you?" I asked Joseph.

"I'm good," he answered. "Tryna keep it together, ya know?" He looked at Jayden who was bundled up to keep him from feeling the cold air. "So, this is your son?"

"Yup, this is Jayden. First, let me introduce you to my husband." Pulling my husband's arm with my free hand, "Lance, this is my brother Joseph. Joseph, this is my husband Lance and our daughter Jayda."

"Nice to meet you, Fam," Joseph greeted with an extended hand."

"Likewise," Lance replied.

"And these are our other kids: Keenan, Lamar, Alanna, and Chantel."

"Nice to meet y'all," Joseph said hugging the girls and shaking hands with the boys.

"What about me, Joey?" Logan snorted. "You're not happy to see me?"

Smiling, Joseph said, "Well, well, well. Lo-Lo!" Joseph and Logan were very close before we were separated as kids. "Damn, Sis, you cut your hair?"

"I had to. I have too many heads to do in my house now so I sacrificed mine. Joey, I want you to meet my husband, Brian and our kids A.J., Amira, Janelle, Aleasha, and Austin."

"Wow! Y'all move down south and breed a whole squad!" Joseph declared.

"That's what I thought," added James who walked up behind Joseph. We all exchanged hugs and hellos and then decided it was enough standing out in the cold so we went inside to find a section to sit in since everyone else pretty much had gone inside.

We walked into the sanctuary and found some seats. Including my brothers, we took up two pews by ourselves. I couldn't stop looking at my grandmother's body lying in the open casket. Everyone else who came in went up to the casket to see her and wept. We sat in the third row from the front and that was good enough for me. My mother, aunts and uncles sat up front. My mother and aunts bawled uncontrollably and that made me close down any emotion that I felt as far as wanting to let go and cry. Logan, Brian, and their kids walked up to our grandmother's casket. They supported Logan as she wept and mourned. I held on to Jayden so tightly I was unaware of his squirming to get out of my lap until Lance whispered, "Honey, give me the baby."

I let my hold of Jayden go and unbeknownst to me I began to tremble. Lance quickly passed the babies to Keenan and

Alanna and put his arms around me.

"Don't make me walk up there, Lance," I whispered.

"I won't," he said. "You don't have to."

"I can't stay here. I can't do this."

"Mo, we're here with you. All of us. You're not alone."

Still whispering I said, "No...no...I can't stay here!"

I bolted out of the pew excusing myself as I passed my family. I walked quickly out of the sanctuary and outside of the church. Lance was in tow.

"Morgan. Morgan, honey, talk to me," Lance requested.

"I can't do this! I can't sit in there and say good-bye! I can't sit in there with a bunch of people who ignored the abuse my mother inflicted upon me and then they chastised my grandmother for raising me! I just can't...I...can't..." and the storm I've been carrying for over 20 years finally poured out from within me. "Everybody in my immediate *ignored* me and Logan! Some of my own cousins badgered us because we were the "white" kids and it didn't help to have the adults crack jokes about us and how we didn't fit in with them. They said Grandmama was wrong for taking us away from our mother; that she was spiteful and hateful toward Belle. Where were they when Belle constantly tortured me? Where were they when Belle starved my sister? Where were they when Belle hit my brother Joseph with an iron for eating her cheeseburger? And where were they when we all had to share a bedroom before we moved to the projects and had to pretend we were sleeping while she was fucking Daniel? Huh?! *Huh?! Where were they????!!!*"

"Baby," Lance said softly and grabbing my shoulders, "I'm sorry you had to go through that. But your grandmother sacrificed a lot for you to make sure you didn't become a product of your environment. She made sure you went to college, had a roof over your head, and food to eat. Most importantly, she gave you safety and security. I understand you're angry and you have the right to be. But what would your grandmother say to you right now? How many times had she told you that you made her proud? Mo, she gave you what your mother didn't and couldn't. She gave you unconditional love and taught you the values of life. It may have taken you a while to get to where you are, but you never steered far away from love. If so, you and I wouldn't be. Now, I promise you sweetheart, you're going to be okay. Let's go back inside and out of this cold air, okay? I got you."

Following my husband's lead, we went back into the church and sat with our children. Since Logan sat directly behind me, I felt her hand on my shoulder.

After the service, we all went to my Aunt Ivory's house on Bedford Avenue. Her house wasn't that big, but somehow well over fifty people were inside eating, talking, and sharing their fondest memories of my grandmother. Joseph, James, Logan and I caught up with each other as well as getting the kids acquainted with their uncles. We all sat in the renovated and furnished basement that was made into a den and discussed how we needed to bond more and build our relationships. Just as we were all on good vibes and expressing our love, in walks...Belle; our mother. Sashaying in her black skirt suit, Belle put on a smile and said, "It's so good to see all of my children together again. Not to mention I get to see my grandchildren."

Breaking the silence, James walked over to her, gave her a hug, and said, "It's good to see you too."

Still smiling as if it was hurtful to do, she asked, "Do any of you need anything else? Something to eat? Drink?"

"Naw, I'm cool," Joseph answered. Everyone else shook their heads no.

"Kids, do y'all want anything?" she asked. Logan signed to Janelle and Amira and they both responded no.

"Oh...okay," Belle said about to walk out of the den. Then she stopped abruptly and said, "Morgan, Logan, Joseph...I know you have hard feelings for me and I'm sorry y'all feel that way. But you're not going to make me look like the enemy here."

Lance queued for our children, Brian, and Brian's children to leave the den and they did just that. I guess he knew they didn't need to be around for that conversation. Once they left out, Joseph asked in his deep and heavy voice, "What do you mean we're making you look like the enemy?"

"C'mon, Son. You and your sisters have separated yourselves from me for years. Even after I've tried to make peace."

Logan stood up next to Joseph and said, "None of this makes sense, Ma. What are you trying to say?"

"Look...I didn't know how to be a mother to y'all. My mother didn't teach me how to love a child."

"That's the biggest bunch of bull!" I yelled. "Nobody knows how to be a parent! It's something you learn internally and instinctively! You either have that instinct naturally or you don't. And apparently you didn't and still don't!"

"How dare you use that tone with me?! You're still my—"

"—I have *never* been your daughter! *Ever!* You may have birthed me, but you are nowhere near being my mother! *Our* mother! A mother doesn't allow her boyfriend to molest her child! A mother doesn't beat up and neglect her two daughters for being high-yellow or let others mistreat them! A mother doesn't disown her son for looking like his father and being abusive to him because his father chose another woman! A mother weathers all of the storms of life and protects her children at all costs!"

Smugly, Belle walked to me until we were eye-to-eye. James

stood closely by. "So, you think you know it all; huh Morgan? You think you know about me, don't you?"

"I know what I need to know and it's helped me be the woman I refused to become by the examples you set."

"You think you grown, don't you?"

"I'm 32 years old. Don't talk to me like I'm a child."

James stepped in. "Ma, let it go."

"James, you watch this one. She got crazy written all over her."

As much as I wanted to snatch that auburn wig off of her head and shove it down her throat, I contained myself with the help of Logan's arms around me and Joseph holding my hand.

"Ma," James began, "leave her alone. Why did you do that? You just said to me four days ago how much you wanted to try and rebuild your relationship with Mo and Lo and you do this? C'mon. Grandmama wouldn't have wanted this."

"Your grandmother stopped me from trying to build a relationship with your sisters! When I got clean, I tried to see them, call them, and spend time with them. She kept telling me no. This is the reason why they are the way they are with me."

"No, Ma, we're the way we are with you because of the foundation you didn't set up for us," Logan stated.

"Not to mention not even giving a damn about me and my situation with my father," Joseph added. "You just let him ship me off to military school at 5 years old!"

"Joseph, I done told you it was for your own good. We were in no shape to raise you," Belle responded.

"So abuse us, ship Joseph off, and make up all your wrong-doings with James?" Logan questioned. "Do you know how that sounds?"

"Logan, how do I make y'all understand that my life was hard when I had y'all? When your grandfather pulled a gun out on me, told me to leave, and leave y'all with them that crushed me."

"So you were being vindictive with us because you were a young, reckless woman with three kids?" Logan asked.

"What is with y'all? I don't owe you explanations for anything. I'm telling you what you need to know. And I'm not going to stand here and be badgered by a bunch of spoiled, ungrateful people," Belle declared

"You're right. You don't owe us anything," I said. "But I'll forgive you because that's what my soul needs to do in order for me to live peacefully. People at fault can never recognize the pain they've inflicted on others, but are quick to point out when someone hurts them. So with that being said, I forgive you for. You're my mother and I'll always have love for you because you were the vessel God chose for me to come into existence. But we have absolutely no need to keep in contact."

Logan, James, and Joseph all looked at me in shock. Stepping back a half an inch, my mother said to me, "If that's what you want; fine. I'll keep my distance from you. Believe it or not, I never meant to hurt you...none of you. I'm dealing with that every day and I can't change what happened in the past. I wanted to start off with a clean and new beginning with all of you. I see that one of you don't want it. Logan...Joseph...where are you with this?"

Joseph looked at Belle and said, "Ma, I'm not gonna lie. Being away from my sisters and little brother was some painful shit. Can't come home for the holidays because I had no home to go to, nobody coming to support me when I made accomplishments or went off to the military and not even having Grandmama like Mo and Lo had her was hurtful. It was like you birthed me and gave me away like I was a mutt. All because my father left you and went with another woman? And let's put this out here on the table now. Daniel wasn't my biological father. You were pregnant with me a month before y'all hooked up."

Logan, James, and I were surprised and felt like a rug was pulled from under our feet.

"What?" Logan whispered.

"Yeah, that's right. Daniel told me all about it in a letter he sent me just before I graduated and went to the Marines. He sent me away because he couldn't stand to see me knowing I wasn't his. How'd he put it? Oh yeah...he already had two kids not his in his life. He didn't want the stress of dealing with three though he said he was cool with it and allowed me to have his last name. You knew he didn't want to deal with me and my sisters as we got older. You sold us out for a piece of—"

"Don't you dare, Joseph!" Belle said.

"Ma," James began. His voice was stressed with pain. "Is all of this true? Me and Joe don't have the same father? And you let my father ship him off to military school?"

"James, there's a lot you'll never understand," Belle replied. "There's a lot that none of you will ever understand. And no matter what I try to say, y'all will never let me live it down."

"Ma," Logan started, "do you understand that because of you Mo and I never knew how to be women? How to have standards with men? How not to get sucked in to a man's lies or games? How to deal with pregnancy and motherhood? We had nobody to teach us! I lived with Aunt Michelle and saw the abuse she endured from her husband and I thought that was normal! I allowed that in my first marriage until I was fed up and my life was in danger. And Mo..."

"Don't, Logan. It's not even worth it," I stated.

I couldn't take anymore of Belle's dry, emotionless, and uncaring explanations of why she inflicted so much pain in our lives so I began to walk away from all of them to find my husband.

"Wait, Mo, where are you going?" Logan asked.

"I'm not standing here listening to this...this...sorry and uncaring explanation on why we had an abusive mother. I'm getting my husband and kids and going back to the bed and breakfast."

"Wait for us, Mo," Joseph requested.

"Oh, so y'all just gonna leave like that?" Belle said.

Joseph turned to our mother and said, "You left us long time ago, Ma. We love you, but it's time for us to continue living our lives without holding on to the pain you've caused us."

"Fine," Belle said quietly. "If that's what y'all want...fine."

I walked upstairs to the kitchen and looked for Lance. I didn't have to look far though. All I had to do was go into the kitchen where there was food and all of my female relatives. Lance came to me with a plate of sweet potato pie smiling.

"Mo, this here is off the chain! You gotta get this recipe."

"Honey, I'm glad you like the pie, but I'm ready to go. Where are my babies?"

"Oh, um your Aunt Grace and Aunt Ivory have them."

"Okay. I'll round up everyone else."

"Wait, Mo. What's the rush? Everything alright?"

"Let's just go...please. I've had enough—"

"—Morgan! Is that you?!" I heard a voice screech. I turned around to see my cousin Katie. The short, cocoa lady smiled from ear to ear and put her arms around me so quick I didn't have time to respond.

"Hey, Katie," I acknowledged. "Long time."

"Yes, I know! Aunt Elaine will be missed. I know how much you loved her and she you. You're looking good in those dreds!"

"Thank you. Um, Katie, this is my husband Lance—"

"—child you late! I already met him, your kids, and his kids! Why don't you ever come home sometimes? We really miss you and Logan; despite the fact she married a white man."

"Geez, Katie!"

"Well you know how our family is. If it ain't black we question it."

Lance started laughing and I glared at him until he stopped.

"I'm sorry, Mo, but that's funny," he replied. "I'm gonna go round up the family."

"Okay," I said.

"Mo, he is *fine*. I mean finer than frog's hair! And his son Keenan...damn!"

"Katie, you're a little too old to be looking at Keenan."

"Girl, you and I are the same age. I bet I could tame that tiger right there!"

"Katie!"

"What? He ain't related to me."

"But he's my step-son."

"And not related to me!"

"You still haven't changed," I laughed.

"Hell naw! When y'all leaving anyway?"

"Sunday morning. It may be tomorrow depending on how this day ends."

"Good. I have one whole day with y'all. We gotta go to The Strip and at least get our dance on. But for now, let me go see my step-cousin and keep it all in the family."

"Katie!"

"What's the problem?" Lance inquired walking behind me with Jayden in his arm.

Exhaling sharply, I said, "Katie is sniffing around for Keenan."

"Ain't she a little old for him?"

I turned and looked at Lance. "Seriously? What about the fact that she's my cousin and he's my step-son?"

"I'm kidding, Baby. I feel you. I'm gonna talk with him about that."

"Thank you."

"Where's Logan?" Lance asked.

"Right here," Logan said. "I'm ready to go also. I just got Brian to round up the kids. James and Joseph are going to hang out with us."

"Cool with me," I stated.

We said our goodbyes to the many relatives that came to my grandmother's funeral and exchanged phone numbers with some of my cousins whom I haven't seen since I graduated college back in 1999. Though this had been a very emotional and trying event for me, I think the biggest obstacle of my life had come at me in full circle and I dealt with it. I recognized a lot of my reckless behavior and emotional dysfunction was from the lack of a stable and loving foundation with my mother. It all made sense to me. The drive for success, wanting to be in control, being afraid to love and receive love, acting out in anger...it all made sense. What I had to do now, was take this chapter of my life and change the outcome; my outcome. I had to be a better woman and that meant I had to be a better child of God, a better wife, mother, sister, and aunt. I just couldn't give up on me and I had to let my God take the reins. However, getting back home and dealing with another chapter of my life had to take place before I could progress into someone better. Unbeknownst to me, the next test of my faith was back in Georgia.

## Chapter Eight

May 14, 2010. Logan, Alanna, Chantel, and Brian's sister Sharon were helping me decorate my backyard for Jayda and Jayden's birthday. The spring breeze was blowing softly as we set up the food table, game tables, and gift table. Lance, Brian, and Brian's brothers Mark and Nick, were off picking up last minute additions for the party favors that we were going to give our guests. Total there were supposed to be 30 tots running around which included some babies from the day care where the twins attend and the children of our cousins Roland and Ramir who were about a few months to two years older than my babies. Keenan and Lamar were unable to come because of finals, but Joseph and James were able to come down and that was a delight in itself.

I went back into the kitchen to get some more plastic wear when I heard my home phone ring. I typically don't answer unknown callers, but this time I picked up my phone and answered.

"Hello?" I spoke into the receiver.

There was a pause for a second before I heard a female's voice say, "Yes, can I speak to Keenan?"

"He's not here at the moment. Can I take a message?"

"Well who's this?" the voice said.

"Whoa...wait a minute, child. You called my phone asking to speak to my step-son. Who is *this?*" I replied.

"My name is Zanaya. I'm sorry...not trying to disrespect your home, but I've been trying to reach Keenan for a while now and he's been ignoring my calls. If I give you my number, can you please have him call me?"

"Sure. Hold on while I get something to write with." I searched in our junk drawer for a pen and a piece of paper. When I got them, I told the girl to recite her phone number for me. I sensed some urgency in her voice and though I swore I'd never get into my step-children's personal business, I couldn't help myself. "Um...Zanaya, right? Can I tell him the reason you need him to call you as soon as possible?"

"Yes...you can tell him I need him to be present to sign my baby's birth certificate in the next six months."

My jaw dropped. Keenan was about to be a father! "Y—yeah...I'll have him call you as soon as I hear from him. Don't worry."

"Thank you, ma'am. Bye," Zanaya said before hanging up. I slowly put the receiver down and clicked the phone off. How in the world was this going to pan out? What was Lance gonna do? Grant it, Lance was 18 when Keenan was born. But the way he is now and have two one-year olds, I don't think he's gonna be too happy to hear he's going to be a grandfather.

"Morgan Brooks! Hello!" Logan said standing behind me. "Child, you look like you've just seen a ghost. What's going on?"

"Logan...I...Keenan...Lance is..." I sputtered.

"What, Mo? What?"

"Some girl...Keenan...baby..."

"Mo, you sound like you're having a seizure. What're you trying to say?"

"Some girl just called looking for Keenan. He's gonna be a father."

Standing back, Logan asked, "Who's gonna be a father?!"

"Keenan! Logan...Keenan is gonna be a father."

With her hands over her mouth and her eyes wide open, I heard Logan say, "Oh...my...goodness. Are you serious?"

I nodded my head.

"Well, you know Keenan's gonna ask for a DNA test, Mo. He's too slick to get trapped like that."

"Wait, Cookie, you didn't try to trap Amari when y'all met in college or when you met Brian. I didn't try to trap Lance."

"Honey, you know as well as I know that there are plenty of young girls trying to get that boy. Hell...even our cousin Katie was trying...and our cousin Ramona's daughter Kenya. Admit it; Keenan is fine as you know what and what's worse is he knows and thinks he's immune to getting a girl pregnant or catching a disease."

"Logan, how do I tell him without pissing him off? You know how Keenan is."

"I don't know, Mo. But you're gonna figure it out. You always do."

Logan carried the rest of the food outside with Sharon's help. I finished gathering everything else and took it all outside. As soon as I got outside, my cell phone rang. After getting the phone out of my back pocket of my jean capris, I clicked the talk button without looking at the caller ID.

"Yes?" I spoke into the phone.

"Hey Mo-Ma," Lamar replied. "I wanted to say happy birthday to my baby sister and brother."

"Aww, how sweet! Of course you can. Hold on a sec." I walked over to the babies who were scrambling around the yard with their uncles Joseph and James playing with a big yellow plastic ball. Once I was able to get them near the phone, I pressed the speaker phone and told Lamar to say it to them. They heard their brother's voice and tried to talk back to him. It was so cute. Then I heard Keenan get on the phone and gave Jayda and Jayden a song for their birthday and they stood around and did their baby dance. After he sang, I said, "Keenan, I need to talk to you for a second."

"Alright," he replied.

I took the phone off speaker and walked toward the back of the house where no one was. As quietly as I could, I said, "Keenan, do you know a girl named Zanaya?"

"Psh, yeah I do. How do you know her, Mo-Ma?"

"She called here looking for you."

"Why? Did she say why?"

"She gave me her number to give to you and—"

"—Naw! I'm not calling that chick! She's crazier than a bat outta hell!"

"Well, Keenan, it looks like you're gonna have to call her because she's saying she's pregnant with your child."

"Huh?! What?! That's impossible! I always strapped up when we got together. There ain't no way I'm her baby's dad, Mo-Ma!"

"Honey, that's something you and her need to discuss. Do you have her number?"

"Nope. I got rid of it when I got rid of her."

"Keenan, you know rubbers do break and can have small tears in them."

"Mo-Ma, I swear she's lying. I kept my own condoms because I know chicks are good at poking holes in the ones they buy. Some will even take one out a trash can and use it later. I wrapped mine up in tissue and took them with me. Mo-Ma, I'm not that baby's father."

"What if you are? Huh? What if? You owe it to yourself to find out. Now, I have her number and I'm gonna text it to you. Whatever you do after that is up to you. And before you ask, I'm not telling your father."

"Thank you!"

"You're welcome. Now...handle your business."

After hanging up with Keenan, I felt drained. I have witnessed so many false paternities and my brother Joseph was a part of that too. But I also know what it's like to not have a relationship as a child with my own father or a positive father figure. It is very important for a child to have that; boy or girl. Though we all want to know where we come from, sometimes it's in the best interest of an impressionable and innocent child to stay away from abuse and confusion that exists within their biological families while they're young. If a child is going to be reared, he or she should be reared positively. All men and women are capable of bringing forth a baby. However, it takes a special man and woman to raise a baby with values.

*************************************************

After the babies' birthday party, Lance and I went out to the movies. One of the best things about having a close network of family is being able to rely on that network at any given time and we were so grateful to Sharon volunteering to keep the babies. We went to a 7 o'clock show and halfway through the movie, I had to use the restroom. I excused myself to find a lavatory. Drinking all of that Mountain Dew did not help me at all.

As I was exiting the ladies' room, I wasn't paying attention where I was walking and bumped into someone. "Excuse me...I..." then I stopped myself. It was Victor. "Hey now," Victor said with a broad smile. "Fancy running into you here. I miss you in class on Tuesdays and Thursdays."

Clearing my throat, I said, "Sorry you miss me."

I was trying to walk back to the theater when Victor grabbed my arm. Startled I turned around and said, "What the hell's wrong with you grabbing me?"

"Morgan, I just wanna talk to you," Victor replied.

"We have nothing to talk about, Victor."

"Oh I believe we do. Now for 10 years I've always wondered what I'd do if I ran into you again. I know what happened with us ended on a sour note, but we were kids."

"You raped me, Victor!"

"And you stabbed me, Morgan!"

"You tricked me into pimpin' out my sister's best friend!"

"And you liked that lifestyle!"

"How did you find me anyway? Social Media? Autumn Reyes?"

"Morgan, I'm a legal analyst for a top television broadcasting network down here and have been here in Alpharetta since we graduated college. I found out you were here years ago through a mutual friend whose daughter receives services at Shining Star. Yeah. She spoke highly of you all of the time; even showed me a picture of you all at the company's banquet. Does the name Quiana Williams ring a bell?"

I was stumped and my mouth dropped.

"Aww, Morgan, don't look baffled. You know it's a small world and I know people just like you do. All I had to do was ask questions until I found you. Quiana and I used to date before your ex-boyfriend Kevin Littleton took her from me."

"She was never yours if another man took her. My husband's waiting on me. Let go of my arm!"

"Not until you tell me why you aborted my baby."

"What are you talking about?"

"Don't play games with me, Morgan. I knew I got you pregnant that day. I knew your cycle like the back of my hand. I intentionally raped you because I wanted you to carry my child. And you killed my baby."

"My...God...you're sick, Victor!" I said snatching away from him.

"Tell me you didn't go to The Pop Shop with Imani...you know...the girl we called Blaze. Tell me you didn't go there."

The Pop Shop was an abortion clinic in Indiana, PA that was set up by a retired gynecologist who serviced high school and college girls.

"What difference does it make if I did or not? I wasn't about to ruin my life like my sister did."

"Ah...so you did."

"Yes. Yes, Victor...I aborted your baby. I had to! My sister already dropped out because she got pregnant. I had a standard to uphold for my grandmother and my late grandfather at the time. I had dreams, goals, and aspirations. I wasn't giving all of that up for a child I wasn't ready for and a man I didn't love."

"Oh...you didn't love me? Really? See that's not how I remembered it. Though you had that fling with Jerome and that so-called relationship with Thomas, I was the only one that understood you; cared for you. I filled the void where they couldn't. But you...killing my baby...not cool."

"So now what? You think I owe you something?"

"How could you be so cold, Mogan? That semester with you was the most meaningful to me. I thought I was winning your heart and you, you played me. I wanted a future with you."

"Remember when I met your parents during homecoming, Victor?"

"Yeah, so?"

"Your parents didn't approve of me. Your mother and father told me that just because my skin was as white as a White woman I'd never be accepted by them because my genetic root was from Africa. That's the reason I didn't get into you like I wanted to."

"Why didn't you tell me?"

"What was the point? You worshipped the ground they walked on and would've eventually dumped me because they told you to."

Looking past his shoulder, I noticed Lance coming out of theater 12 of the movie we were watching and my heart jumped. "Victor, my husband is walking up behind you. Please."

Smiling a crooked and sinister smile, Victor said, "This ain't over, Morgan."

Walking up with concern, Lance stood at my side and put his arm around my waist. Talking to Victor, Lance questioned, "Everything alright here? Who are you?"

"Victor. I'm an old friend of your wife's from college," he answered.

"Is that right?" Lance asked then looking at me for reassurance.

"Yes, honey, Victor and I used to go to IUP."

"Oh. Well, Mo, you're missing the movie. C'mon. Nice to meet you, Victor," Lance said escorting me back to the theater.

"Likewise," Victor said snidely.

As we walked toward the theater, Lance pulled me closer to him and said, "What was that all about? And Morgan for the love of everything holy, don't lie to me or try to cover it up."

"Victor and I were friends and it ended on a sour note," I answered.

"How close were y'all?"

"What?"

"Girl, you heard me? Y'all slept together, didn't you?"

"Baby, that was in college."

"It doesn't matter to him, Mo. What I felt coming off of him was something ugly. I don't trust that guy. Stay away from him."

We got back to our seats and finished the movie. I couldn't enjoy it anymore and I knew Lance was making himself finish the film. All of a sudden, he sprung up in his chair, turned toward me and whispered as quietly as he could, "*That* was the dude from college? Who you were involved with in the escort gig??"

Whispering, I said, "Honey, not here."

Slamming his body back in his seat, Lance was quiet for the rest of the movie. On the way home though, that was a different story.

"Mo, how long have you known that this guy has been down here?" Lance asked as he drove angrily.

"I don't know. Since last summer," I answered.

"How could you not tell me this? Don't you think I deserved to know that your pimp moved to our town?"

"First of all, he was never my pimp! Second of all, what would've been the point in telling you?"

"Oh I don't know, Morgan! Maybe I could've done surveillance, made sure that this clown didn't bother you anymore, anything! This whole thing stinks to high heaven!"

"Lance, you don't have to worry about him."

"Why is that? Huh? You gonna try to wipe him out too?"

"Now wait a minute! That's not fair!"

"No, Morgan, what's not fair is constantly having you damn skeletons appear in my life and in our children's lives."

"Constantly? You make it seem like I invite pain into our home intentionally on a daily basis."

"Look at your track record! You good for a couple of months, and then here comes a bone! Mo, I swear on everything I love you're my everything. But damn!"

"So...my perfect, flawless husband is finally telling me the truth? You're admitting that you don't want this anymore?"

"Stop playing the victim, Morgan! That's not what I'm saying. All I'm saying is you don't trust me to protect you. You don't trust me to love you. And...you don't trust me to be your husband."

"I'm done talking to you about this, Lance."

"Just as you always are when you're called out."

Without thinking of the ramifications that would follow, I took the rest of my slushy from the theater I had and dumped it in Lance's lap as he drove.

"Mo! What the—"

"—Shut up and drive us home! I'm sick of you belittling me every chance you get when you don't like something or someone of my past appearing! You asked me to marry you! You said you'd love me for better or worse! You knew I had a fucked up life before we came together! But you chose to sign up for this! *You* did! Now I hope your balls will tell your brain to chill out and get us home!"

Without anything more to say, Lance drove home. The whole time I kept thinking about how I was trying to keep my darkest parts of my life locked away and no matter how I try to keep them locked away, they always seem to surface. There were times when I tried to find fault in my husband or tried to find dirt on him just as a get-back and it never worked. This man had told me everything about his upbringing, his relationship with Sharayne, and even about the ladies he got involved with before we became exclusive. His only hang-up is his obsessive compulsive behavior with the order he keeps his things and how he likes lines in grass when it's cut.

When we arrived home, it was well after 9pm. The babies were down for the night, Chantel and Alanna were in their rooms, and Sharon was watching a movie. We thanked her for keeping the babies and she went home. I went into my bedroom and pulled out my night clothes as I got ready to shower before bed. I pulled my dreds up in a ponytail and stepped out on the balcony of the bedroom. I looked up at the stars as the nighttime air hit my skin. Our backyard was private and was surrounded by weeping willow trees and a creek. The fireflies danced and I inhaled and exhaled deeply. Lance crept up behind me and put his hands on my shoulders. He spun me around aggressively, looked me deep in my eyes, and said, "Morgan, I love you." Before I had a chance to respond, he pulled me close to him and shoved his tongue down my throat. I was not in the mood for his kisses and I tried to pull away from him. "Stop, Lance." I demanded, but he ignored me. He grabbed me forcefully into his body and kissed my neck and it frightened me. He's never thrown himself at me like that and it reminded me of when Victor attacked me. "Lance...I...said...stop!" And with the word stop, I slapped him in the face as hard as I could. Stepping back toward the balcony door, I sized him up. "What has gotten into you?!" I asked.

"You," Lance said. "You have gotten into me, under me, and through me. You won't make love to me, I can't get any affection out of you, you're acting as if you don't want me around for nothing but to raise our kids and make appearances."

"So you'd rape me?"

"What? No! Morgan, how could you say—"

"—Victor raped me in college, Lance! He *raped* me! And what you just did—"

"—Mo, I'm sorry! I didn't...I..."

"Just leave me alone!"

I stormed back in the bedroom and scurried in the bathroom and locked the door to make sure he didn't come in.

I made myself some bathwater with lavender bath oil. While the water ran, I cried. Why was this happening to me? Why couldn't I have a peaceful life without inflicting pain on my family? On myself? When I turned the water off and was about to get into the tub, I felt a presence in the bathroom with me and it was all too familiar. My mirror image with the onyx eyes stood and waited for me. This time instead of a sinister and creepily wide smile, her lips were closed. I looked at her and looked at her and then I walked to the mirror. With a very distorted voice, my reflection said, "You're separating yourself from me. Why?"

"I don't know what you're talking about," I replied.

"Your heart is growing soft. You have more love in your

heart than before. I can't exist without pain," the reflection said.

"You were never supposed to exist in the first place," I stated. "All I ever wanted was love and to be loved. I'm tired of living with contempt in my heart for everything and everyone. I'm tired of the nightmares and flashbacks. I want to be free and therefore, my dark reflection, I release you. You are no longer a part of me."

The Reflection's eyes turned from black to white and then to my natural eye color. I saw a figure move away from the mirror and I felt my soul lifted. My demon was gone.

I undressed and slid into the bathwater and let the almost hot water seep into my pores. The smell of lavender was soothing and relaxing. I put my iPod on and listened to some music. As I did, I fell into a deep sleep and wasn't aware that I had fallen off to sleep and into my nightmare.
\*\*\*\*\*\*\*\*\*\*\*\*\*\*\*\*\*\*\*\*\*\*\*\*\*\*\*\*\*\*\*\*\*\*\*\*\*\*\*\*\*\*\*\*\*\*\*\*\*\*\*\*\*\*

February 1999. It was only a few months before I graduated from IUP. I was on my way to my elective course when I was approached by Logan's best friend Imani Jones.

"Hey, Morgan," Imani said carrying her very heavy book bag on her frail back. She had on some white earmuffs that matched her white down coat and Timberland boots. Her blemish-free face stood out as it was the color of the outside of an almond.

"What's good, Blaze?" I asked still walking to my class.

"Um, I need to talk to you. About what happened with you and Victor."

"What business is that of yours?" I asked.

"Look, I know we're not all working together anymore. Especially after that ordeal I had back in October. But I'd still like to be friends."

"Yeah...that's cool," I said. "Look, I don't mean to be rude, but my class starts in five minutes and I don't have a lot of time."

"Sure, sure, go ahead. Thanks, Morgan. Please tell your sister I'm gonna call her one day this week."

I nodded my head and waved as I walked to my class. When I got there, everyone was pretty much seated and waiting for the professor to come in. When she finally did arrive, I couldn't concentrate on the lecture because my stomach was flipping and flopping. I felt myself start sweating and a familiar nauseous feeling surfaced all over me. I quickly got up and ran out of the classroom. Though I tried to make it to the bathroom, I heaved in the first trash can I saw. I was so embarrassed because there were other people walking in the hallway at the time. I got to the bathroom and cleaned myself up. At the time, I was thinking I had a stomach virus because for two weeks off and on I'd been vomiting at various times during the day and evening. It was time I saw a doctor so after that class I went to the student health center and saw a nurse practitioner on duty. When I told her my symptoms, she asked me when my last cycle was, I told her it was three weeks prior. She looked at me and told me just as a precaution, I should take a pregnancy test. I scoffed at the idea. There was no way I could've been pregnant. I had my period every month, I wasn't gaining weight or had crazy cravings, and I wasn't feeling bloated; all of the things Logan said she felt. I gave a urine sample to the nurse and waited for her to come back and tell me she was wrong and I was experiencing a stomach virus that was just taking longer to run its course. The nurse came back in the exam room, looked at me as if I was a kid whole stole candy, and told me I was pregnant. I felt my heart sink and my head spin. I collapsed on the floor of the student health center.

When I came to, the nurse practitioner and the doctor on duty placed me on the exam table. They checked my vitals and asked me if I felt I needed urgent care. I was given brochures and resources for first-time mothers. I thanked them half-heartedly and walked out of the student health center and back to my apartment. When I got back, Patrice was there with her girlfriend and boyfriend watching a movie.

"Hey, Morgan! I ordered some pizza," Patrice announced.

"Hi, everyone," I greeted. "Thanks, Patrice. But I'm gonna pass on the pizza."

"Too bad. More for me," she joked.

I went to my room and dove on my bed. I can't be pregnant! I hadn't had sex with anyone; or so I thought until it dawned on me that incident with Victor before winter break. There was no way in hell I'd have this baby! Besides, I had a whole life's plan ahead of me and having a baby wasn't in my plan. I called Imani Jones because a while back, she had an abortion. When she finally answered her phone, I was relieved.

"Hey, Blaze. It's Morgan," I said into the receiver of the phone.

"Hey, hey. How are you?" she asked.

"I'm perplexed right now," I replied. "Listen, I'm not gonna beat around the bush. What's the name of the place you went to get that procedure done? You know...the abortion."

There was a pause on the other end. "The Pop Shop. Why?"

"Where's it located?"

"Behind the shopping center off of Millay Circle. Mo, what's going on?"

"Can you take me? I don't know anyone else here with a car that I trust."

"Oh...oh...damn. You sure you wanna do this?"

"Blaze, I got too much riding on me if I don't. Will you go

with me or not?"

"Um...yeah...sure. It's only open on Wednesday and Thursday mornings and it's $200 cash up front."

"No problem. What time do I need to be ready?"

"I'll pick you up at 6:30am tomorrow morning. The doctor only takes the first five females without an appointment."

"Alright. I'll be ready. See you in the morning." After hanging up with Imani, I lied on my bed and sulked. Never in my mind did it occur to me that Victor raping me would've caused me to get pregnant. Stuff like that didn't happen in my mind except in Lifetime movies.

The next morning, I was dressed and outside of my apartment building at 6:30am and Imani was right on time. I got into her Cavalier and we took off. As she drove, I thought about how I used to really like Victor. I didn't want to admit it, but he was right. He filled the void of Thomas' absence though we were in a long-distance relationship and attending two different colleges.

"Morgan? You alright?" Imani asked.

"Yeah. I'm good. I just want to get this over with," I answered.

"If you don't mind me asking, is this Victor's baby?"

"Why ask if you know I'd mind?"

"Well, I mean, everyone speculated y'all were an item even though you both denied it. Besides working together, you two were damn near inseparable until that big fight y'all had at his apartment."

"Swear to me you'll never tell anyone. Not even my sister."

"Okay. I swear."

"Victor raped me and yes I'm pregnant by that horrific act."

"Aw, Mo, I'm so, so, sorry. I didn't know."

"And this stays in this car and between us. Do you

understand me? So help me if I find out you told anyone..."
"Yeah; understood."

We arrived at The Pop Shop 15 minutes after we left my apartment building. There were already three girls waiting in line; two of them looked no older than 14. It was about 15 degrees outside and the bone chilling cold seeped through my coat and clothes. Imani went into her coat pocket and lit a cigarette. As she puffed on it, she looked around our surroundings.

"Wow, I thought I'd never come back here," Imani declared.
"Really? Why?" I questioned.
"My experience and reason is a little different than yours. One of my regular clients, Evan, was into some off the wall type stuff. Toys, acting, even threesomes. One particular night, he invited his boy to join in. I thought nothing of it because that was an extra buck fifty. I was high off of acid and didn't have too much care about anything that night. We did some straight pornographic type stuff. Needless to say, I didn't make either one of them strap up and they both released in me. When I learned I was knocked, I came here. It was a shame for me because I was feeling my regular dude and he told me if I stopped with that life, he'd take care of me. We talked about kids, commitment, and being exclusive. But when I got pregnant and didn't know who the dad was, there was no way I could serve him again nor be willing to give up that life for Evan. Not until Roger damn near killed me. Shit...that was my wake up call. By the time I healed and got my mind right, my Evan was long gone outta here and on the next bus to New Orleans. That was my man. Had I changed my ways, I'd be free from this bullshit."
"Blaze, I had no idea."
"Nobody did; except your sister. She kept telling me to move on and get my life together. But you knew what it was

like to get that cash, Mo. It was a drug all in itself."

"Yeah. I know. Listen...I...I apologize for contributing to that pain."

Taking her final drag off the cigarette, Imani said, "No need to apologize. I signed up for that life before you became a part of it."

The office lights came on and the door opened. We walked inside and signed our names on the clipboard that sat on the desktop where the receptionist sat. The clinic had wood panel walls, old corduroy furniture, and smelled like mothballs. The doctor's accreditations were hanging in the waiting area as well as plenty of reading material and brochures. We each had to pick up a questionnaire to answer questions about ourselves; demographics, health history, etc. Once we completed it, we had to take it back to the rooms with us. The nurse called the first girl back. Ten minutes later, she called the second. Ten minutes after that she called the third. Ten minutes after the third, it was me.

"I'll be here waiting for you," Imani said.

I followed the nurse who looked very unhappy to be there. Her sunken cheekbones made her nose a focal point of her face and her long, red hair was pulled up in a bun. She opened room number 9 and directed me to sit on the table. Very uncaring and almost rude, the nurse said in a dry tone, "Okay, here's your gown. Undress yourself, but leave your bra and socks on. Make sure the gown is open in the back. There's a plastic cup for you to leave a urine sample with the directions attached to the cup. Once you're done, push this button to signal you're ready. We'll come in to do your vitals and take an ultrasound which is to determine how far along you are. If we find that you are over 12 weeks, we will not, under any circumstances, do this procedure. Any questions?"

"No," I answered.

"Fine. Press the red button over here on the wall next to the door when you're done and someone will be in."

Like the wind, the nurse quickly exited the room. I started to undress and put on the hospital gown leaving on my bra and socks. I went in the bathroom that was joined to the procedure room I was in to put a urine sample in. After I urinated in the cup, I washed my hands, sealed the container, and came back to the room. I pushed the button next to the door as instructed and I climbed onto the table. Within a couple of seconds, the same nurse came back into the room, hastily took a dropper, dipped in into my urine sample, and put some drops on the pregnancy test stick. As she done that, she wheeled the ultrasound machine over toward me. The doctor came into the room as the nurse was setting up the machine. He was tall and kind of stocky with a receding hairline of gray hair. He had pasty white skin and a clean shaven face that displayed very thin lips, wrinkles around his gray eyes, and a hooked nose. The sight of him gave me chills and not in a good way.

"Hello, I'm Dr. Norway," he introduced in a groggy voice with breath that smelled like old coffee. He glanced at the pregnancy stick and said, "Looks here like you're positive and expecting. I would say congratulations but you're not here to celebrate. Now..." he said as he picked up and put down my questionnaire, "Morgan...I'm going to insert a wand in your vagina to get an ultrasound."

"Wait," I said, "I thought those are done on top of my stomach?"

"Only if you're about three to four months," he replied. "Right now, the baby may be too small to be seen on the belly wand."

"Oh," I said.

"Now, I need you to scoot your bottom to the edge of the

table and place your feet in the stirrups."

I did as I was instructed. After preparing the wand with a condom and ultrasound jelly, Dr. Norway inserted the tool inside and it was very uncomfortable. He kept the monitor facing him so I couldn't see the screen. In a way, I wanted to see the ultrasound. At the same time, I'm happy I didn't.

"Hmm," Dr. Norway said. "Looks here you...are...somewhere near 8 to 9 weeks. If you'd waited any longer, this procedure wouldn't have happened. Well, not in my facility." Dr. Norway quickly snatched the wand out of my bottom, told me to sit back for a while, and walked over to his tool tray before stepping out of the room. The nurse pulled out and hooked up the vacuum aspiration machine along with a tank of laughing gas.

"Now, you can opt to have the laughing gas or go natural," she snorted. Her whole attitude was messing with my mind and I couldn't take it anymore.

"Ma'am, what is with you?" I questioned her. "Why do you have to have such a bad attitude and customer service? At the end of the day, regardless of what I'm doing here or if you don't agree with the choice I'm making, you don't need to handle me like I'm a street urchin."

Without missing a beat, the nurse said, "Well, you're right. I don't like what you or any other female come here to do. If you were a little smarter or more careful, this wouldn't be taking place. Besides, there's always adoption or just learning how to lie in the bed you made. I pray God have mercy on all of you."

Just as quick as she came at me, I said, "You know...you're right. A lot of us *females* should be more careful. But how can you protect yourself from someone you know who rapes you? What about the young girls being victim to incest? Or have medical issues that cause them to not be able to carry the baby? At the end of the day, you're here to do a job; not preach or pass judgment. We're all gonna have to face God on judgment day. Until then, don't stand here on your high horse and give me or any other woman who walks in here a hard time about what she chooses to do on the side of the living. Now, can you be a little more professional and less personal?"

Without further comment on the topic, she said in a strained voice trying to keep her composure, "Would you like to have the laughing gas or go natural?"

Positioning myself on the table, I said, "I'll take the gas." As she was giving me the laughing gas, Dr. Norway and another nurse walked in. In a low voice, he directed her to the vacuum aspiration machine. He rewashed his hands, put on latex gloves and sat on the stool. "Okay, Morgan, scoot your bottom back down to the edge of the table and place your feet back in the stirrups," Dr. Norway instructed and I followed. The moody nurse gave me the laughing gas and told me to inhale and exhale deeply and slowly. As I done that, I heard the machine start up.

"Okay, Morgan. I'm going to dilate your cervix first and then I'm going to insert the aspiration tube into your vagina. This will be over in no time," Dr. Norway said. I kept inhaling and exhaling the laughing gas and even though it was supposed to sedate me, I felt *everything*. He dilated my cervix and it felt like he was taking a hot pointed metal iron and stabbing it profusely. I gripped the sides of the table I lied on until my knuckles turned white. After what felt like forever, the machine whirred on and he began the procedure. My cervix and uterus vibrated and felt like it was being torn out of my body. With a tear rolling out the corner of my eye and down to my ear, I silently prayed to God that under no circumstance would I ever, ever, have another abortion and whatever punishment or consequence I was going to endure from this, I'll take it.

Several minutes later, Dr. Norway was done. I got up off the table, got dressed, and received instructions from the nurse who was rude to me most of the day. I took my instructions and walked out to the waiting room. I didn't see Imani and started to wonder where she went to. I sat down on the same couch I did when we arrived in the waiting room and waited for her for ten minutes. She finally came back in the facility and her eyes were wide open as if she saw a ghost.

"Um, h-hey, Morgan," Imani stammered. "Y-you okay?" Imani was very twitchy.

"I'm fine," I replied. "I'm ready to go. What's going on with you? Did you drop some acid?"

"No! No...I just came from getting some...breakfast. And it's cold outside so...yeah...let's go."

We walked out to her car and got in. I felt so sore and I was actually relieved it was over. But something was going on with Imani and I had to know what. When we got to the streetlight, I noticed a car behind us that looked very familiar. I turned to look but couldn't get a good look because of the cracked, tinted back window in Imani's car. I looked as much as I could on the side view mirror and kept looking until the car passed us and went the other way. I could've sworn it was Victor, but there were a lot of people driving blue Chevy Caprice Classics.

"Hmm, that looked like Victor," I said baiting Imani.

"Girl, you know he don't get out on Wednesday mornings," she stated. "Remember?"

"Yeah...you're right," I said. Victor would work at his legit job Monday and Tuesday nights from 11pm to 7am as a security guard. "Thank you, Blaze."

"No problem. A girl's gotta do what she gotta do; at all costs."
\*\*\*\*\*\*\*\*\*\*\*\*\*\*\*\*\*\*\*\*\*\*\*\*\*\*\*\*\*\*\*\*\*\*\*\*\*\*\*\*\*\*\*\*\*\*\*\*\*\*\*\*

"Morgan! Morgan! Honey, open the door!" Lance yelled banging on the bathroom door. The problem was I couldn't hear him because I was submerged under water. He must've known something was wrong because he found the emergency key and opened it. When he saw me under water, Lance quickly snatched me up, dragged me out of the tub, and lied my body on the floor.

"Baby, why are you doing this to me?" Lance said in a panic as he checked for my vitals. Being certified in CPR, he noticed I had a weak pulse. He gave me mouth to mouth until I coughed up and spit out water. I gasped for air and coughed hard. When I opened my eyes, I looked up at my husband confused.

"Morgan...Mo..."Lance whispered and kissed my forehead. "I'm sorry. Please don't do this anymore."

"Do what?" I asked. "What happened?"

"You fell asleep in the tub again, didn't you?" he asked.

"I guess I did. I sat in the water, turned my iPod on, and I guess I nodded out."

"Mo, baby, you scared me! I thought you were trying to kill yourself after what happened out on the balcony."

"What? No...I love myself to much to take my own life on purpose."

"Mo, was that true what you said? About that guy at the movies you went to college with?"

"Yes. He raped me because he wanted to purposely impregnate me. And...when I found out he did lay his seed, I killed it."

Shocked with my reply, Lance said, "He raped you so you can have his baby? The guy that you used to work for as a madam in college?"

"Yes."

"And you had an abortion?"

"Yes."

"Morgan...I'm at a loss of words."

"Lance, I've been so ashamed of my past that it was always hard for me to tell you the truth. I didn't want you to judge me or look at me any differently which would wanna make you divorce me or never marry me in the beginning."

Smiling, Lance said, "Morgan Taylor Brooks, God brought you to me for a reason. The way we came together may not have been right, but I knew you were the one for me. Your past is your past. I'm here to help you heal. As your husband, it's my job to protect you, care for you, and see you through your worst of times. C'mon, let's get you dried and dressed. I'm going to take you to the ER to get checked on and make sure you don't have any water left in your lungs."

"Lance, I'm sorry for being such a difficult wife. Please forgive me. I love you."

"Forgive me for being a man in physical desperation."

## Chapter Nine

November 2010. Keenan agreed to meet with Zanaya to take a DNA test after dodging and ignoring her calls and text messages and this particular day was the day he was going to find out if he fathered a child. He still never told his father about the baby because he was unsure if the baby was his or not. He arrived at the DNA clinic near the Fulton County hospital nervous and a bit angry. As he walked through the glass doors, he signed in at the front desk and was instructed to have a seat. When he turned around, he saw Zanaya holding a baby girl and for the first time in his life, he felt scared and insecure in himself. Zanaya cradled her baby and nuzzled her little face. As Keenan slowly walked toward them, he noticed how beautiful Zanaya was. Her caramel skin glowed and her dark brown eyes sparkled between her thick, long natural eyelashes. Her full lips had a hint of lip gloss and her eyes were lined with fine smoke eyeliner. Her short hair was cropped and spiked and her nails were perfectly manicured. He was also impressed with how she was able to get her body back in the same size it was before she was pregnant.

When she looked up, she saw Keenan standing in front of her and though angry and feeling betrayed, was caught off guard with Keenan's handsomeness and physique.
Clearing his throat, Keenan said, "You mind if I have a seat?"
"Sure," Zanaya said in her soft voice.
Keenan removed his coat and sat down. He couldn't help but glance at the little infant who was a little over a month old. "She's...beautiful," he stated.
"Thank you," Zanaya answered.
"So, uh...if this test comes back showing I'm her father,

what do we do?"

"We'll figure it out. I'm not going to make you be a part of my daughter's life if you don't want to be in it. I know how much you enjoy your bachelor life and I don't want her to suffer from it."

"Zanaya, I wouldn't walk away from her."

"How do I know that? You walked away from me, ignored me, and moved on without nothing short of an explanation of why. What did I ever do to you, Keenan?"

"Z, you didn't do anything. It's just...I...I just..."

"Yeah...you just nothing. Keenan, if you weren't into me, why'd you lead me on? I had to find out by your brother's girlfriend you were seeing other girls."

"Lead you on? Really, Z? I didn't lead you on. I told you up front we were just hanging out and I wasn't looking for a relationship. Answer this though, how'd you get pregnant by me if I was always strapped?"

"What! Keenan...are you serious?!"

"Yeah, I'm serious!"

"There were three times when the condom broke."

"And I had my backup and put another on!"

"But you pre-released and that's all it takes!"

"Whatever, Z. Let's change the subject."

"Yeah...let's."

Before they could talk about anything more, an employee called their names at the front desk. Both Keenan and Zanaya walked up to the front desk and were directed to a booth down the hall. They sat down and waited for one of the DNA techs to come meet them. When the technician finally arrived, Keenan was a ball of nerves though he didn't display it.

"Okay," the technician said as he sat down in front of them. "Zanaya Forbes and Keenan Brooks, correct?"

"Yes," Zanaya replied.

"Yeah," Keenan answered.

The technician opened the folder and looked over the results carefully. Keenan started to tap his foot and Zanaya noticed. "Well, Keenan you are 99.87% a match as the baby's father," the technician announced.

"So, what does that mean?" Keenan asked.

"It means you are a father," the technician said. "I would say congratulations, but I don't know if this is good news or bad news for you." The technician handed the folder to Keenan and Keenan hesitantly took the folder. The technician said as he stood to leave, "Y'all have a good day." Zanaya kissed her daughter and said to the baby, "I told you I would bring your father to you."

Keenan sat still and looked over the DNA results. Knowing at that moment he had to tell his father was going to be hard because Lance had set standards and expectations for him and his siblings. Zanaya stood up to leave and started to walk away. Keenan snapped out of his daze and said, "Hold up, Z." He stood up to face her and took a good look at the baby girl. "What's her name?"

Smiling, Zanaya said, "Akila Grace."

"Hmm. Can I hold her for a second?"

With a little reservation, Zanaya agreed. Keenan carefully held his daughter in his big biceps. He just looked at her without saying a word. He studied her face, skin, and the little strands of black hair he saw peeking from under her hat.

"Akila," he said, "I'm your father. My name is Keenan Dwayne Brooks. I'm the oldest of six kids and am currently a senior in college at Kennesaw State. I'm gonna do everything I can to do right by you; I promise."

\*\*\*\*\*\*\*\*\*\*\*\*\*\*\*\*\*\*\*\*\*\*\*\*\*\*\*\*\*\*\*\*\*\*\*\*\*\*\*\*\*\*\*\*\*\*\*\*\*\*\*\*\*\*\*\*\*\*

At home, Lance and I were planning for our two year anniversary trip in December. We wanted to plan ahead, but life kept popping up. The twins were more active, Chantel was able to walk without a walker and we celebrated her big achievement, Alanna was getting ready for prom, and Lamar decided to study theology to become a pastor. Sharayne moved to Oregon with a guy she met on the internet and was no longer calling her children or Lance. Brian and Logan had gone to France for their 5 year anniversary back in September and the excitement and fun they had was written all over them when they came back. Needless to say having four more children in this house for a whole week was an adventure all its own and Lance was fortunate enough to be at work while I had to find time to work at home. My brother Joseph re-enlisted in the Marines and my brother James graduated with honors from Duquesne University majoring in accounting. He decided to stop working for Port Authority and moved to Atlanta to work for top celebrities...and to be closer to me and Logan.

While sitting in the den discussing travel plans to the Bahamas, in walks Keenan. He looked a little antsy as he approached his father and I already knew what it was about considering he told me about taking the DNA test two weeks ago.
"Ahem, uh, Dad? I need to talk to you," Keenan said.
"Sure, son," Lance responded without looking away from the computer screen. "What's on your mind?"
"Uh, Dad, I need your undivided attention."
Lance looked up at his son and glared trying to read Keenan's disposition. "Alright. You have my attention."
Standing as firmly as he could, Keenan said, "Dad, first let me say that everything you taught me, I never took for granted. I understood everything you've instilled in me since

you and my mother split and Lamar and I came here to live with you permanently. You teaching me how to be a man is something I'll never be ungrateful for. I'm going to graduate college and I'm going to continue to go after my career in law. However...along the way of me getting to where you guided me to, my ego took over. And...I thought I was untouchable and too good for many women."

Keenan paused and Lance sat looking perplexed. But he didn't interrupt his son.

"Dad...I...I uh...hold on a second."

Keenan walked out of the den and walked down the hall until he was out of sight. When he came back in, he was not alone. Holding a little person wrapped in a lavender, fleece blanket and walking alongside a young, beautiful lady, Keenan steadily found his wording. I looked at Lance and his eyes said a thousand words.

"Dad, this is Zanaya," Keenan introduced.

"Hello, Mr. Brooks," Zanaya said. Lance got up away from the computer desk and stood right next to it. I was shocked by his demeanor because he'd typically walk over to someone and shake their hand. Not this time.

"Hello, Zanaya." Lance said calmly.

"And...this is Akira Grace," Keenan stated. "She's my daughter."

"Your...daughter?" Lance questioned.

"Yes, Sir."

Lance was speechless. He crossed his arms and put one hand over his goatee and stroked it.

"Zanaya, could you give my son and I a moment or two?"

"Yes, Sir," she replied. She went to reach for Akira when Lance said sternly, "No, no. Let my son hold his daughter. Mo, could you please accompany this young lady to the living room?"

"Yes I can," I responded. Walking toward Zanaya, I directed her to the living room.

Lance walked over to the door and closed it and told Keenan to sit in a chair. He thought carefully about what he was going to say to his son and when he did, he let everything flow.

"Keenan, do you have any idea what you're up against now? The amount of responsibility, time, and selflessness that comes with being a father? Didn't you hear anything I told you about what it was like for me to become a father at 18 years old?"

"Dad, I know what you've told me and I know how hard it was for you to raise me."

"Not only that, but how naïve I was and brought your brother into the world a year and a week later? Followed by your sisters three and four years after that? How I had to work two jobs to care for y'all for years? What's your plan, son? What are you going to do for this baby, huh? How are you going to clothe and feed her? Keep health insurance for her? Are you going to go to her doctor's appointments? Help her mother with day care expenses? Are you going to set her up with a college fund? Tell me, Son...how are you going to care for this baby? See...you can't throw all of the responsibility on that young lady in there because she didn't make this angel on her own; you helped. It's more than just all the cutesies of a baby. You are going to be the first man in this baby girl's life. You're going to have to set the standard for her. How she should behave like a lady and how not to get involved with men who'll disrespect and abuse her. You're going to have to be the example and do right by her mother. Now, I'm not saying y'all have to get married, but you're going to have to do right by this baby's mother."

"Dad, I know all of what you're saying is true. I didn't plan on this, but I'm not going to walk away from her. I'm going to take care of her; I promise. I'm not going to lie, Dad, I'm scared. I'm gonna pick up some more hours at the job and do what I've seen you do all my life which is take care of your kids."

Walking over and placing his hand on Keenan's shoulder, Lance said, "It's a natural and good feeling to be scared. That means you have the heart and the drive to raise a child. But son...couldn't you have waited until I was in my 50s? I mean...I'm 39 years old! 39! I have 1 year old twins and a 33 year old wife. Damn!" Sitting next to Keenan, Lance took Akira from her father and held her. She opened her eyes and both men said hello to her.

"I can't believe I'm a...a...a grandfather," Lance remarked. "But damn it if she isn't beautiful."

Smiling and agreeing, Keenan said, "She definitely is."

"You sure she's yours?"

"Yeah. I got the DNA test results today. Dad, at first I was thinking Zanaya was lying or trying to trap me. But we talked on the way over here and I realize that I was too arrogant and stuck on myself that I didn't think for one second about her or any other woman I slept with. I messed up."

"Keenan, you didn't mess up. You thought with the wrong head and the fact that you've always been a ladies magnet you became conceited and thought you were above the possibility of becoming a father. I got your back, Son. Just as my dad did for me with you."

Sitting in the living room, Zanaya and I were getting to know each other. Though she had a very soft voice, I could tell she had some fire in her. With the exception of the color of her eyes, she reminded me of the model Nicole

Murphy.

"So, how do you think it's going in there, Mrs. Brooks?"

Laughing a little, I said, "It should be going just as it should."

"I hope Mr. Brooks isn't upset."

"Well, you can't blame him for feeling that way. He had expectations for all of his children; especially Keenan because he's the first son and the oldest. One thing I want you to know is despite all of this, your baby will be well loved and supported by this family."

Toddling in from their bedroom were Jayda and Jayden. I guess Blue's Clues stopped playing on their DVD.

"Oh my goodness! They're so cute!" Zanaya stated.

"Thank you," I said. "These are my babies and Keenan's one year old baby brother and sister, Jayda and Jayden.

"Oh my goodness. They have a niece a year younger than them!" Zanaya replied.

"Yes...they do. Awkward, isn't it?" I asked.

"Well, kinda. But these things happen, right?"

"Well this is a first for Lance's family." Jayda walked over to me and said, "Blue."

"Excuse me, Zanaya. I'm gonna go put on the other DVD for them."

As I was walking down the hall with the twins to their room, Lance, Keenan, and the baby were walking toward the living room. Lance winked at me and I knew that everything was going to be okay.

Joining Zanaya in the living room, Lance, Keenan, and the baby all took a seat. Typically the mother or mother figure grills the young women in their son's life. Not our house. Lance grilled everyone who came in contact with his older children. Sitting back comfortably and with confidence in his chair, Lance looked at Zanaya and asked, "So to my understanding this wasn't anything planned between you two?"

Softly Zanaya answered, "No, Sir. We were careful, or trying to be careful, every time. I want to make this perfectly clear to both of you. I didn't plan on this and I didn't conjure this up just to have permanent ties with Keenan. I don't believe in abortions and I couldn't imagine giving away my baby. As I told Keenan, if I have to, I'll raise her on my own. However, I know there would've come a time in her life where she would ask the question of who her father is and whenever he was ready to be a part of, I'd direct her to him if I could. I don't care about child support, visitations, none of that. I know Keenan is doing his thing and I'm doing mine."

"Oh, so you have a lot of answers and solutions?" Lance questioned. "Hmm. So, you're okay with my son bringing your daughter around other women?"

Keenan stopped kissing Akila and looked up at Zanaya.

"Well, um, I mean, he can see whomever he wants," she answered.

"We know that, Z, but what my father's asking is will you trip if I have my daughter around someone I'm dating?" Keenan interjected.

Shifting in her seat, it was very obvious that Zanaya didn't like that idea at all.

"Let me ease your mind, Z. When I have a date or whatever, I'm not bringing Akila around them. She's gonna be here with me and my family only. It's not healthy or respectful."

Trying not to show her enthusiasm, she said, "Okay."

"Hold on," Keenan began. "Where's your head at with dating other guys? I mean, it was obvious you would've had a problem with me bringing our daughter around other women. So, is this gonna be a double standard; I can't but you can?"

"Oh, no, not at all," Zanaya answered. "If I get into a serious relationship down the line, I want him to first meet Akila's father. I have to do the opposite of what my mother did with me when I was growing up. She brought all types of men around me and my brothers and it was weird. My father has always been a part of my life, but it's just different when your mother dates a bunch of guys who try to step in and be involved when they're not going to be around for the long run. With me being the only girl with five brothers, I was exposed to too much. So, no; I'm not going to have her around other guys."

"And when I get into a serious relationship? What do you expect?" Keenan inquired.

"I expect the same standard and respect, Keenan."

"Well, I'm glad all of this has been established and in front of witnesses," Lance said standing up. "Zanaya, it's a pleasure meeting you. Thank you for bringing Akila to meet us."

"Sure. Thank you for having us," she replied.

"C'mon, Mo, we have to finish planning our anniversary trip."

"Right behind you," I said. "Nice to have met you, Zanaya."

"Same here, Mrs. Brooks."

When Lance and I left the living room and went back to the den, Zanaya and Keenan continued talking so Keenan could get acquainted with his daughter. Lance and I entered the den and he closed the door behind us. Walking over to the lounge, he exhaled sharply and put his hands over his face. I sat next to him and rubbed his chest.

"Mo, I'm a grandfather. A 39 year old grandfather."

"Well, Honey, this is nothing for me. My great-grandmother was having kids when her two oldest kids had children. My grandmother was 38 years old when I was born."

"I know you're trying to comfort me and I appreciate it. But...look at me. I'm in shape, in good health, don't have gray hair, and I have one year old twins. When I go places, people with her, people are gonna talk."

"Lance, your son is 21 years old. What could they possibly say and why would you let it affect you? How do you think your mother felt when you had him at 18?"

"She was already in her 40s!"

"Lance. Honey, you're a sexy grandfather. Don't let the public eye dictate how you feel. Though you're disappointed with Keenan, it was written all over you the joy you had holding her."

"Ha, ha, ha. You think you know me, huh?"

"Yes. I'd like to think I know you very well."

"Well, you do know that you're a grandmother now? You do know that she's gonna call you Grandma!"

"Oh, hell naw! I'm not claiming that title! That's you and Sharayne all day."

"Wait, wait, wait. They all call you Mo-Ma. It ain't my fault you're only 12 years older than your oldest step-son. You claim my four children as yours. You've said it yourself. You introduce them as your kids."

"Yeah, but—"

"—Unh, unh, Mo! We're in this together! Ha, ha, ha! You're a 33 year old grandmother! Ha, ha, ha!"

"Well...she's gonna have to call me something else."

Lance pulled me closer to him and kissed my cheek. "We're in this together, Mo. I love you for loving me and my children."

"I love you for loving me and allowing me to be a part of their lives." We gave each other a long and sensual kiss.

When we pulled away from each other, Lance said, "Well, there goes the plan of adding more babies to the family."

"Huh? Excuse me? Who was having more babies and for what family?" I asked. "Lance, I told you I was done after that whole ordeal I went through with the twins."
"I'm just joking, Mo. C'mon. Let's finish planning our anniversary trip."

## **Finale**

I love my family more than anyone may recognize. My first year of marriage was something I'll never forget because I had to face my past. The garbage I carried with me for years took a toll on my heart and soul and almost killed my spirit. Losing my grandmother was the worst thing that's ever happened to me despite the emotional, sexual, and physical abuse inflicted on me as a child. That pain I carried with me was the root cause of my dysfunction for many years because I refused to let it go. But what do you do when you have a husband that refuse to give up on you? You submit to him and I submitted to my husband and I allowed him to love me and see me through that embarrassing and horrific pain.

I was so blessed to have the opportunity to reconnect with my brothers Joseph and James. To this day, we talk every week and always see each other on holidays. By the spring of 2011, my whole family prospered in so many ways. Logan and Brian continue to be a force to reckon with. Brian's moved up with the Georgia Department of Education and Logan became a national spokeswoman on the importance of supporting deaf and hard of hearing resources, education, jobs, and other services through her company she built from home; *Deafinitely Awesome.* Being a hearing mother of two deaf children and having a hard of hearing husband, Logan sought after her dedication on the importance of family and community support for the hearing impaired.

Alanna graduated high school with honors and earned a full scholarship for journalism at Clark University and Chantel has found her place as a senior in high school. Though she's not ever going to be 100% again physically,

Chantel spends her time mentoring some of the kids in her school and neighborhood about the dangers of doing drugs and drinking alcohol. Lamar continues to be at the top of his class for theology at Shorter University, where he transferred to once he became dedicated to serving Christ. Jayda and Jayden; my twins. What can you say about two year old twins except their cute and steadily growing? I look at them and love them as much as I can. Finally, I come to Keenan. He graduated with a bachelor's in criminal law and was seeking the master's program. He always made time for his baby girl, Akila Grace, and actually...the baby slowed him down with his womanizing. Though he and Zanaya remained friends, they always put their child first and came together as a unit when it was time.

Yes...2009 and 2010 were the years I grew up. Thank God I didn't have to do it alone.

## **<u>Prelude to Reflecting as Morgan Brooks</u>**

"Lance, I don't feel right about this whole ordeal with moving from Georgia. I mean...we're doing fine here."
"Mo, we gotta move to Charlotte. You've come so far emotionally. You don't need another set back and we need to be closer to my Mom and Dad right now."
"But what about what I want? Didn't you think of how this will affect the twins? They're going to flip if they don't get to see Akila, their cousins, and their brothers and sisters."
"We've been doing what you want for a while now. Right now I need you to be with me on this. Besides...I don't think it's a good idea for us to hang around here. You know what happened to Victor could follow us for life and I don't want that following us or our kids."
"Victor got what he deserved, Lance."
"I have to protect my family, Morgan. I have to protect y'all."
Walking back inside of the house, Lance closed the patio door and went into the den. I stayed outside and looked up at the dusky sky. Maybe it was a good thing for us to move. It's just we have so much vested in being in Georgia. Our careers, owning this home, the older children in college and making their marks in life...not to mention my sister and brother James living here. Yet I understand where my husband is coming from. He being a state officer and having to keep vital information about what happened to Victor from the district attorney is not a good look. Somehow, we have to leave without making things look very suspicious. So Charlotte, NC....here we come.

Made in United States
Orlando, FL
07 May 2022

17622531R00117